SWAN SONG

Robert Bruce Montgomery was born in Buckinghamshire in 1921. After graduating from St John's College, Oxford in 1943 he was a member of a famous literary circle including Kingsley Amis and Philip Larkin. Under the pseudonym Edmund Crispin, he wrote nine detective novels and forty-two short stories. In addition to his reputation as a leader in the field of mystery genre, Montgomery was a successful concert pianist and composer, most notably penning the score for the well-known *Carry On* series.

Montgomery became a regular crime-fiction reviewer for the *Sunday Times* from 1967, contributing to many periodicals, newspapers and edited science-fiction anthologies. After the golden years of the 1950s he retired from the limelight to live in Totnes in Devonshire until his death in 1978.

Also in this series

EDMUND CRISPIN

Swan Song

COLLINS
CRIME
CLUB

COLLINS CRIME CLUB

An imprint of HarperCollins*Publishers*
1 London Bridge Street
London SE1 9GF
www.harpercollins.co.uk

This paperback edition 2018

2

First published in Great Britain by
Victor Gollancz 1947

A catalogue record for this book is
available from the British Library

ISBN 978-0-00-822803-3

Typeset in Sabon by Palimpsest Book Production Ltd, Falkirk, Stirlingshire
Printed and bound by CPI Group (UK) Ltd, Croydon CR0 4YY

MIX
Paper from
responsible sources
FSC™ C007454

This book is produced from independently certified FSC™ paper
to ensure responsible forest management.

For more information visit: www.harpercollins.co.uk/green

My dear Godfrey,

You're not, I fancy, an habitual reader of such murderous tales as this, and in the ordinary way I should be decidedly shy of dedicating one of them to you. But a book with a background of *Die Meistersinger* – well, what else could I do? It was you who first introduced me to that noble work (in the days when the sum of my musical activity consisted in trying to evade piano lessons), and our mutual admiration of it is not the least of the many bonds of friendship between us. Accept the story, then, for the sake of its setting, and as a foretaste of the day when Wagner's masterpiece returns to Covent Garden – without, let us hope, any of the dismal impediments which beset it in the following pages.

Yours as ever,

E. C.

Devon, 1946

Chapter One

There are few creatures more stupid than the average singer. It would appear that the fractional adjustment of larynx, glottis, and sinuses required in the production of beautiful sounds must almost invariably be accompanied – so perverse are the habits of Providence – by the witlessness of a barn-yard fowl. Perhaps, though, the thing is not so much innate as a result of environment and training. This touchiness and irascibility, these scarifying intellectual lapses, are observable in actors as well – and it has long been noted that singers who are concerned with the theatre are more obtuse and trying than any other kind. One would be inclined, indeed, to attribute their deficiencies exclusively to the practice of personal display were it not for the existence of ballet-dancers, who (with a few notable exceptions) are most usually naïve and mild-eyed. Evidently there is no immediate and summary solution of the problem. The fact itself, however, is very generally admitted.

Certainly Elizabeth Harding was aware of it – perhaps only theoretically at first, but with a good deal of practical confirmation as the rehearsals of *Der Rosenkavalier* ran their course. She was therefore relieved to find that Adam Langley was considerably more cultured and intelligent, as well as

1

more svelte and personable, than the majority of operatic tenors. It was her intention to marry him, and plainly the quality of his mind was a factor which had to be taken into account.

Elizabeth was not, of course, in any way a cold or calculating person. But most women – despite the romantic fictions which obscure the whole marriage problem – are realistic enough, before committing themselves, to examine with some care the merits and demerits of their prospective husbands. Moreover, Elizabeth had gained by her own talents a settled and independent position in life, and this was not, she had decided, to be abandoned improvidently at the behest of mere affection, however strong. She therefore reviewed the situation with characteristic thoroughness and clarity of mind.

And the situation was this, that she had fallen explicably and quite unexpectedly in love with an operatic tenor. In her more apprehensive moments, in fact, infatuation suggested itself to her as a more accurate term than love. The symptoms left her in no possible doubt as to her condition. They showed, even, so strong a resemblance to the tropes and platitudes of the conventional love-story as to be vaguely disconcerting. She thought about Adam before she went to sleep at night; she was still thinking about him when she woke up in the morning; she even – the ultimate degradation – dreamed about him; and she hurried to the opera-house to meet him with an eagerness quite inappropriate to a reserved and sophisticated young woman of twenty-six. In a way it was humiliating; on the other hand, it was decidedly the most delightful and exhilarating form of humiliation she had ever experienced – and that in spite of a sufficiency of practice in love and rather too much theoretical reading on the subject.

How it came about she was never able clearly to remember, but it seems to have happened quite suddenly, without gestation or warning. One day Adam Langley was an agreeable but undifferentiated member of an operatic company; the next he shone alone in planetary splendour, amid satellites grown spectral and unreal. Elizabeth felt, in the face of this phenomenon, something of the awe of a coenobite visited by an archangel, and was startled at the hurried refocusing of familiar objects which such an experience involves. *'Fallings from us, vanishings . . .'* She would certainly have resented this gratuitous upsetting of her normal outlook had it not been for the unprecedented sense of peace and happiness which it brought with it. 'Darling Adam,' she murmured that night to a hot and unresponsive pillow, 'darling ugly Adam' – a form of endearment which its object would probably have greatly resented had he known of it. There was more to the same effect, but such ecstasies make a poor showing by the time the printer has finished with them, and the reader will either have to take them for granted or imagine them for himself.

The epithet was as a matter of fact slanderous. Adam Langley was entirely presentable, being thirty-five years of age, with kindly, regular, undistinguished features, thoughtful brown eyes, and a habit of courtesy which served admirably as a defence to his natural shyness. His chief defect lay in a certain vagueness which amounted sometimes to the appearance of aimlessness. He was trustful, modest, easily startled, and innocent of all but the most venial misdemeanours, and though at one time and another he had been moved to a gentle and – if the truth is to be told – rather clumsy amorousness, women had played no very important part in his peaceful and successful life. It was perhaps for this reason that he remained for so long totally unaware of Elizabeth's feelings for him. He regarded her, at all events in the first instance, simply as a writer who had gained admittance to the rehearsals of *Der Rosenkavalier* in order to study the operatic background required for an episode in a new novel.

'But *schön*!' Karl Wolzogen hissed at him during a break in one of the piano rehearsals. 'If she could only sing – ah, my friend, what an Oktavian!' And more out of courtesy than because he was impressed by Karl's enthusiasm – which tended, in truth, to be indiscriminate – Adam studied Elizabeth properly for the first time. She was small, he saw, exquisitely slender, with soft brown hair, blue eyes, a slightly snub nose, and eyebrows which were crooked and hence a trifle sardonic. Her voice – she was speaking at this moment to Joan Davis – was low, vivid, and quiet, with a not unattractive huskiness. Her lipstick had been applied with a rare competence, and of this Adam greatly approved, since it seemed to him that the majority of women must perform this operation in front of a distorting mirror or during an attack of St Vitus's Dance. She was dressed soberly and expensively, though with a little too much masculinity for Adam's taste. And as to character? Here Adam became a little bogged. He liked, however, her disciplined vivacity and her poise – the more so as there was no hint of arrogance about it.

Subsequently he was in the habit of attributing their marriage to the independent purposes of Herren Strauss and Hofmannsthal. The chief singing parts in *Der Rosenkavalier* are for three sopranos and a bass. Adam, being a tenor, had been fobbed off with the small and uninteresting role of Valzacchi, and this left him, at rehearsals, more often unoccupied than not. It was inevitable that he and Elizabeth should drift together – and so far, so good. But here an obstacle presented itself, in that it never for one instant occurred to Adam that Elizabeth might wish their relationship to rise above the level of disinterested affability on which it had begun. On this plane he obstinately remained, blind to winsomeness and affection, deaf to hints and innuendoes, in a paradisaically innocent condition of sexlessness which exasperated Elizabeth all the more since it was obviously natural and unconscious. For a time she was baffled. An open declaration of her feelings, she saw, was far more likely to put him on guard than to encourage him – and moreover her own characteristic reserve would invest such a declaration with a perceptible air of incongruity and falsity. It says much for the semi-hypnosis in which her mind was fogged that the obvious solution came to her only after a considerable time: plainly some third person must be found to mediate between them.

They had no mutual acquaintance outside the opera-house, and inside it there was only one possible choice for such a delicate mission. A woman was indicated – and a woman, moreover, who was mature, worldly, sensible, and friendly with Adam. So one evening, after the rehearsal was over, Elizabeth went to visit Joan Davis (who was singing the part of the Marschallin) at her flat in Maida Vale.

The room into which an elderly, heavy-footed maidservant ushered her was untidy – so untidy as to suggest the aftermath of a burglary. It soon became apparent, however, that this was the normal condition of Miss Davis's belongings. The maid announced Elizabeth, clucked deprecatorily, made a half-hearted foray among a welter of articles on the sideboard, and then departed, tramping vehemently and muttering to herself.

'Poor Elsie.' Joan shook her head. 'She'll never reconcile herself to my slatternly ways. Sit down, my dear, and have a drink.'

'You're not busy?'

'As you see' – Joan waved a needle, a shrivelled length of silk, and a mushroom-shaped object constructed of wood – 'I'm mending. But I can quite well go on with that while you talk to me . . . Gin and something?'

They chattered of commonplaces while they sat and smoked their cigarettes. Then, with some misgiving, Elizabeth broached the reason for her visit.

'You know Adam,' she began, and was taken aback at having made so idiotic a statement. 'That is to say—'

'That is to say,' Joan put in, 'that you're rather taken with him.'

She grinned disconcertingly. She was a tall, slender woman of about thirty-five, with features which, though too irregular for beauty, were yet remarkably expressive. The grin mingled shrewdness with a cynical, impish vivacity.

Elizabeth was frankly dismayed. 'Is it as obvious as all that?'

'Certainly – to everyone except Adam. I've thought once or twice of letting even him into the secret, but it hardly does for an outsider to interfere in these things.'

'As a matter of fact' – Elizabeth blushed slightly in spite of herself – 'that's exactly what I came here to ask you to do.'

'My dear, what fun. I shall enjoy it thoroughly . . .' Joan paused to reflect. 'Yes, I see now that it's probably the only way. Adam is not, in our grandparents' phrase, a "person of much observation". But he's a good-hearted creature, all the same. Blessings to you both. I'll tackle him tomorrow.'

And this she did, carrying Adam off, in a suitably idle moment, to the green-room. What she had to tell him took him completely unawares. He expostulated, feebly and without conviction. Subsequently Joan left him to meditate upon her words and returned to the rehearsal.

His initial surprise gave place almost at once to an overwhelming sense of gratification – and this by no means for reasons of vanity, but because an obscure sense of dissatisfaction from which he had recently suffered was now entirely dissipated. For him, too, there was a refocusing, as though the pattern of a puzzle had at last become apparent – become, indeed, so self-evident that its previous obscurity was almost incomprehensible. Beatitude and embarrassment clamoured equally for recognition. Ten minutes previously he had regarded Elizabeth as a pleasant acquaintance; now he had not the least doubt that he was going to marry her.

He was recalled to the stage, and there participated with decided gusto in the discomfiture of Baron Ochs von Lerchenau.

But when actually confronted with Elizabeth his shyness got the better of him. During the week that followed, indeed, he went so far as to avoid her – a phenomenon which filled Elizabeth with secret dismay. She came to believe, as the days passed, that the news of her feelings must have offended him, though as a matter of fact the reason for his unsociability lay in a sort of coyness, for which he severely reproached himself, but which for some time he was quite unable to overcome. In the end it was his growing impatience with his own puerility which brought him to the point. It happened towards the close of the first dress-rehearsal. Bracing himself – in a fashion more appropriate to some monstrous task like the taking of a beleaguered city than to the wooing of a girl whom he knew perfectly well to be fond of him – he went to speak to Elizabeth in the auditorium.

She was sitting, small, demure, cool, and self-possessed, on a red plush seat in the centre of the front row of the stalls. Framed in the large rococo splendours of the opera-house like a fine jewel in an antique setting. Tier upon gilded tier of boxes and galleries, radiating on either side from the royal box, towered into the upper darkness. Callipygic Boucher cherubs and putti held lean striated pillars in a passionate embrace. The great chandelier swayed fractionally in a draught, its crystal pendants winking like fireflies in the light reflected from the stage. And Adam paused, daunted. The *mise-en-scène* was by no means appropriate to the intimate things which he had to say. He consulted first his watch and then the state of affairs on the stage, saw that the rehearsal would be over in half an hour at most, and invited Elizabeth out to a late dinner.

They went to a restaurant in Dean Street, and sat at a table with a red-shaded lamp in a stuffy downstairs room. A small, garrulous, mostly unintelligible Cypriot waiter served them. Adam ordered, with stately deliberation, some very expensive claret, and Elizabeth's spirits rose perceptibly. Since it was obvious that the well-intentioned nagging of their waiter would be unpropitious to confidences, Adam deferred the business of the evening until the arrival of coffee forced the waiter at last to go away. He then embarked on the subject overhastily and without sufficient premeditation.

'Elizabeth,' he said, 'I hear – that is to say, I understand – that is to say that my feelings – what I mean is—'

He stopped abruptly, dumbfounded at so much feebleness and incoherence, and drank the whole of his liqueur at a gulp. He felt like a man who has incomprehensibly lost his nerve on the middle of a tight-rope. Elizabeth experienced a transient exasperation at being kept for so long in suspense; certainly the omens were favourable, but one could not be *completely* sure . . .

'Adam dear,' she replied gently, 'what on earth are you trying to say?'

'I am trying to say,' Adam resumed earnestly, 'that – that I'm in love with you. And that I should like you to marry me. To marry me,' he repeated with unwarranted ferocity, and sat back abruptly, gazing at her with open defiance.

Really, thought Elizabeth, one would imagine he was challenging me to a duel. But oh, Adam, my darling, my unspeakably shy and precious old *idiot* . . . With the utmost difficulty she resisted the temptation to throw herself into his arms. She soon observed, however, that the Cypriot waiter was once again looming, toothily affable, on to their horizon, and decided that the situation had better be dealt with as quickly as possible.

'Adam,' she said with a gravity which she was far from feeling, 'I wish I could tell you how grateful I am. But you know, it isn't the sort of thing one ought to decide on the spur of the moment . . . May I think about it?'

'Any more liqueur, eh?' said the waiter, materializing suddenly beside them. 'Drambuie, Cointreau, Crème-de-Menthe, nice brandy?'

Adam ignored him; now that the worst was over he had recovered much of his self-possession.

'Elizabeth,' he said, 'you're being hypocritical. You know perfectly well that you're going to marry me.'

'Green Chartreuse, nice Vodka—'

'Will you go away. Elizabeth, my dear—'

'You like the cheque, eh?' said the waiter.

'No. Go away at once. As I was saying—'

'Oh, pay the bill, darling,' said Elizabeth. 'And then you can take me outside and kiss me.'

'Kiss 'er 'ere,' said the waiter, interested.

'Oh, Adam, I do adore you,' said Elizabeth. 'Of course I'll marry you.'

'Nice magnum of champagne, eh?' said the waiter. 'Congratulations, sir and madam. Congratulations.' Adam tipped him recklessly and they departed.

For their honeymoon they went to Brunnen. Their rooms at the hotel overlooked the lake. They visited the Wagner-museum at Triebschen, and Adam, in defiance of all the regulations, played the opening bars of *Tristan* on Wagner's Erard piano. They purchased a number of rather *risqué* postcards and sent them to their friends. Both of them were blissfully happy.

They stood on their balcony gazing across the water, now amethyst-coloured in the fading light.

'*How* nice,' said Elizabeth judicially, 'to have all the pleasures of living in sin without any of the disadvantages.'

Chapter Two

The marriage would have been no more noteworthy than ten thousand others had it not been for a third party who was obliquely involved.

Edwin Shorthouse was singing Ochs in *Der Rosenkavalier*. Like Adam, he became acquainted with Elizabeth during the rehearsals. And he, too, fell in love with her.

'Love', as used in this connexion, is largely a euphemism for physical excitement. To the best of everyone's knowledge, Edwin Shorthouse's affairs with women had never risen above this plane. His habits suggested, in fact, a belated attempt to revive the droit de seigneur, and his resemblance to the gross and elderly roué of Strauss's opera was sufficiently remarkable for it to be a subject of perpetual surprise in operatic circles that his interpretation of the role was so inadequate. Possibly he himself was uneasily conscious of the similarity, and felt the basic stupidity of Hofmannsthal's creation to be a reflexion on his own way of life. Sensitivity, however, was not Edwin Shorthouse's most outstanding trait, and it is more likely that his aversion to the part was instinctive.

There may have been something more than mere sensuality in his attitude to Elizabeth. Certainly it is difficult, on any other hypothesis, to account for the active malevolence which Elizabeth's marriage to Adam aroused in him. Joan Davis held the view that it was his vanity which was chiefly concerned. Here was Edwin (she said); coarse-grained, middle-aged, ill-favoured, conceited, and almost continually drunk; and here, on the other hand, was Adam. The choice, to anyone but Shorthouse himself, must have seemed a foregone conclusion: to him it had undoubtedly been a wounding blow.

'But don't worry, my dears,' Joan added. 'Edwin's concern is with the female form divine – not with particular women. As soon as another shapely girl comes along – and the world's full of them – he'll forget his tantrums.'

Elizabeth herself suggested frustration as the cause of Shorthouse's immoderate annoyance. She had not seen a great deal of him at rehearsals, though whenever they met he had been markedly attentive.

'I noticed that,' said Joan. 'He was always "undressing you with his eyes", as the absurd phrase has it.'

Elizabeth agreed. But – she added – it had been difficult to deal with this attitude until the evening when Shorthouse had made efforts to transfer his somewhat cheerless imaginative pastime to the realm of actuality.

'Naturally,' Elizabeth concluded demurely, 'I didn't encourage him . . . Hence, as I say, he's frustrated. That's the answer.'

Adam had yet another theory. In his opinion, Shorthouse was really in love; within his opulent and unprepossessing frame, Adam maintained, there burned the flame which had destroyed Ilium and held Antony in sybaritic bondage by the Nile. 'In other words, l'amour,' said Adam. 'More Levantine than spiritual, I agree, but, none the less, the genuine article.'

There seemed, in fact, to be no wholly satisfactory solution, and for a time they contemplated the phenomenon with no stronger emotion than a mild interest. Eventually, however, it became tedious, and at last irritating. Adam was obliged to be fairly often in Shorthouse's company, and there are few things more exacerbating than an attitude compounded of sneers and snubs – and an attitude the more disconcerting, in this case, because of the real hatred which lurked behind it. In the early days of the engagement, moreover, Adam became aware that sundry vague and discreditable rumours concerning him were going the rounds of his acquaintance, and in one case they found such ready acceptance that he was estranged without explanation from a family with whom he had been for years on the friendliest possible terms. In his innocence Adam did not at first connect Shorthouse with this new affliction, and it needed a chance remark to enlighten him. Even so he controlled himself and carried on as if nothing had happened. Adam had some respect for his work and was determined if possible, to avoid complicating it by an open rift with Shorthouse.

The honeymoon, which followed the *Rosenkavalier* production, gave him a respite, and when he and Elizabeth returned from Switzerland to set up house in Tunbridge Wells they were too much occupied with organizing their joint *ménage* to worry about anything else. Shorthouse, presumably, would be simmering down by now; and luckily, their engagements kept the two men apart until November, when both of them were signed up for *Don Pasquale*. Adam went to the first rehearsal with mild apprehension, and returned perplexed.

'Well?' Elizabeth demanded as she helped him off with his coat.

'The answer is in the affirmative. Edwin would seem to be cured. All the same . . .' Adam, who had just removed his hat, absent-mindedly put it on again. 'All the same . . .'

'Darling, what *are* you doing? Was he friendly? You don't sound at all sure about it.' They went into the drawing-room, where a huge fire was burning, and Elizabeth poured sherry.

'He was friendly,' Adam explained, 'in the most overpowering fashion. I don't like it. In the old days Edwin's notion of friendship was to bore one perennially with rambling, pointless anecdotes about his professional experiences. He no longer does that – with me, anyway.'

'Perhaps he's ashamed of himself.'

'It's scarcely likely.'

'I don't see why not. He can't be quite devoid of humanity. Presumably he had a mother.'

'Heliogabalus had a mother. We all had mothers . . . What I mean to say is that there's something artificial about this change in Edwin, it's decidedly insincere.'

'But better, one supposes, than open warfare.'

'I don't know,' said Adam dolefully. 'I'm not at all sure about that. It's the kiss of Judas, if you ask me.'

'Don't be melodramatic, darling, and above all, don't slop your sherry on to the carpet.'

'I never noticed I was doing that,' said Adam.

'In any case,' Elizabeth went on, 'I don't see what High priest Edwin can have betrayed you to.'

'Levi, perhaps.'

'The only qualification Levi has for the part is his race. And anyway, he'd as soon get rid of Edwin as you.'

'You're perfectly right, of course.' Adam frowned. 'Well, I'll see how things turn out. Have you got any news?'

'A commission, darling, and a very profitable one. By the afternoon post.'

'Oh? Congratulations. A new novel?'

'No, a series of interviews for a Sunday paper.'

'Interviews with whom?'

'Private detectives.'

'*Detectives?*' Adam was startled.

Elizabeth kissed him, a little absently, on the tip of the nose. 'You've still got a lot to learn about me, my precious. Didn't you know that my first books were works of popular criminology? I'm generally supposed to understand something about the subject.'

'And do you?'

'Yes,' said Elizabeth. 'I do . . . Unfortunately it'll involve a certain amount of gadding about, and I shall have to settle down with *Who's Who* and write a lot of tiresome letters tomorrow morning. Do *you* know any private detectives?'

'There's one.' Adam spoke rather dubiously. 'A man called Fen.'

'I remember. There was some business about a toyshop, before the war. Where does he live?'

'In Oxford. He's Professor of English there.'

'You must give me an introduction.'

'He's very unpredictable,' said Adam, 'in some ways. Are you in a hurry with these articles?'

'Not specially.'

'Well,' said Adam, 'there's this Oxford production of *Meistersinger* in the new year. If it suits you, we'll get hold of him then.'

The rehearsals of *Don Pasquale* passed off without incident. Shorthouse, without actually seeking Adam's company, maintained his curious affability whenever circumstances made a meeting inevitable. And there came a time when he even went so far as to apologize for his earlier behaviour.

It was immediately after the second performance. Adam had lingered for a few minutes in the wings arguing with the producer about some minor awkwardness which had arisen during the evening, and on entering his dressing-room he was surprised to find Shorthouse there, inspecting, or possibly on the point of purloining, a half-empty jar of removing-cream. This, however, he returned hastily to its place when Adam appeared. He was wearing a voluminous dressing-gown and was still powdered, painted, and be-wigged for the name part of the opera, and Adam supposed that he had run short of removing cream and, their dressing-rooms being adjacent, had decided that this was the simplest way of replenishing his supply. It soon appeared, however, that removing-cream must be, at the most, only a subsidiary reason for his visit.

'Langley,' he said (and the air at once became aromatic with gin), 'I'm afraid you've no reason to be fond of me. The fact is, I didn't behave very well over your marriage.'

Adam, embarrassed, made a dull grunting sound. Shorthouse seemed to find this inspiriting, for he went on, with rather more confidence:

'I came here tonight to apologize. To apologize,' he repeated, sensing perhaps a certain bareness in his original statement. 'For my ill-mannered behaviour,' he added explanatorily after some thought.

'Don't think about it,' Adam mumbled. 'Please don't think about it. I'm only too glad—'

'We can be friends, I hope?'

'Friends?' Adam spoke without enthusiasm. 'Yes, of course.'

'It's very generous of you to take it so well.'

'Don't think about it,' said Adam again.

A silence fell. Shorthouse shifted from one foot to the other. Adam removed his wig and hung it with unnecessary deliberation on the back of a chair.

'Good house tonight,' said Shorthouse.

'Yes, very good. They seemed to be enjoying themselves very much. They laughed,' Adam pointed out, 'quite a lot.'

'Of course, it's a brilliant piece.'

'Brilliant.'

'But I suppose from your point of view – that's to say, there *are* better parts than Ernesto.'

'Oh, I don't know. I've got *Cercherò lontana terra* in the second act.'

'Yes, so you have . . . Well,' said Shorthouse, 'I'll go and get some of this muck off my face.'

'Are you out of cream? I thought I saw—'

'No, no, thanks very much. I was only wondering what kind you used. Well, I'll see you tomorrow.'

'Yes,' said Adam helplessly. 'See you tomorrow.'

And Shorthouse lumbered from the room, leaving Adam greatly relieved at his departure. As he changed, Adam pondered Shorthouse's sudden regeneracy. He continued pondering it all the way back to Tunbridge Wells. Arrived home, he narrated the events of the evening to Elizabeth.

'Removing-cream?' said Elizabeth indignantly. 'He wasn't trying to pinch that new jar I bought for you?'

'No,' Adam reassured her. 'The old one. Yours was still in my coat-pocket. All the same, I shall keep my dressing-room locked from now onwards.'

'Well then, the whole ridiculous business is over.'

'I suppose so. But you know, my dear, I still don't trust

the man. He's quite capable of playing Tartuffe if it suits his book. I'm not sure, if it comes to that, that he isn't capable of murder.'

Adam spoke carelessly. But he was to find soon enough that Edwin Shorthouse was by no means unique in this.

Chapter Three

Adam and Elizabeth travelled up to Oxford on a raw, bleak afternoon late in January. The sky was pigeon-grey and the wind chilling. Adam, fretful at the possibility of hoarseness, was wound up in mufflers, but luckily their trains were adequately heated. From Oxford station they took a taxi to the 'Mace and Sceptre', where they had reserved rooms. Adam stood about and smoked while Elizabeth unpacked and put away their things. Afterwards they went downstairs to the bar, where they were pleased to find Joan Davis, sipping a dry Martini at one of the glass-topped tables.

From her Adam learned various details of the *Meistersinger* production.

Edwin Shorthouse was to play Sachs; the Walther and Eva were of course Adam and Joan; Fritz Adelheim, a young German, had the part of David, and John Barfield that of Kothner.

'And this man Peacock, who's conducting,' said Adam. 'Have you met him?'

'My dear, yes. Very young but utterly charming. This is his first Big Chance, so you must forget all about what you did under Bruno and Tommy, and cooperate zealously.'

'But is he any *good*?'

'That remains to be seen. But I don't think Levi would have put him in if he weren't. Levi has quite an eye for operatic conductors.'

'Who's producing?'

'Daniel Rutherston.'

'As melancholy as ever, I don't doubt. And Karl is régisseur?'

'Yes. Very cock-a-hoop about it. You know what a fanatical Wagnerian he is. Come to think of it,' said Joan, 'I shan't be sorry to get back to Wagner now the war-time interdict has lifted . . . Why *was* there an interdict, anyway?'

'It's a highbrow axiom,' Adam explained, 'that Wagner was responsible for the rise of Nazism. If you want to be in the fashion you must refer darkly to the evil workings of the *Ring* in the Teutonic mentality – though as the whole cycle of operas is devoted to showing that even the gods can't break an agreement without bringing the whole universe crashing about their ears, I've never been able to see what possible encouragement *Hitler* can have got out of it . . . But you mustn't get me on this subject. It's one of my hobby-horses. You've been abroad, Joan, haven't you?'

'In America. Playing *Bohème* and dying of consumption five times weekly. As a matter of fact, I nearly died of over-eating. You should go to America, Adam. They have food there.'

The three of them passed an agreeable evening together and went early to bed. At ten o'clock next morning piano rehearsals began. Beneath an obstinately cinereous sky Adam and Joan walked to the opera-house in Beaumont Street.

While, in general, the English do not erect opera-houses if they can avoid it – preferring commonly such witty and ennobling occupations as Betty Grable and the football pools

– Oxford has recently provided a notable exception to the rule. It stands on the corner of Beaumont Street and St John Street, at the side nearest to Worcester College, and is built of Headington stone. The foyer glows with a discreet, green-carpeted opulence. About it are ranged busts of the greater operatic masters – Wagner, Verdi, Mozart, Gluck, Mussorgsky. There is also one of Brahms – for no very clear reason, though it may perhaps be a tribute to his curious and fortunately abortive project for an opera about gold-mining in the Yukon. The auditorium is comparatively small, but the stage and orchestra-pit are capable of dealing with the grandest of grand opera. The stage equipment is replete with complex and fallible devices, and a menagerie of mechanical fauna inhabits the property-rooms. The dressing-rooms, too, are more luxurious than is usual; the two floors on which they are situated are even served by a small lift.

With such amenities, however, Adam and Joan were not for the moment concerned. They made their way to the stage door, and thence, directed by an aged janitor, to one of the rehearsal rooms.

Most of the others had already arrived, and were grouped round the grand piano. Apart from this, and a number of chairs constructed principally of chromium piping, the place was very bare. Its sole concession to aesthetic decorum was a lopsided photograph of Puccini, markedly resembling the proprietor of an Edwardian ice-cream stall.

Adam was introduced to Peacock, who proved to be a quiet man of about thirty, conventionally dressed, tall, thin, and with a prematurely sparse provision of red hair. Adam liked him immediately. Among the others present were Karl Wolzogen, a wiry little German, preternaturally energetic despite his seventy years; Caithness, at the piano, a dour and laconic Scot; Edwin Shorthouse, exhaling nostalgically the fumes of last night's gin; and John Barfield, the Kothner. The remainder of the cast were not intimately concerned in the events which followed a fortnight later, and need not be specifically mentioned here. Most of them Adam knew, for the number of operatic singers in England is not large, and they are frequently thrown together.

The rehearsal went as well as such rehearsals do go, and it was pleasing to find that Peacock knew his business. Edwin Shorthouse took direction with such unaccustomed meekness that Adam became suspicious. He remained uneasy, indeed, as long as the piano rehearsals lasted. Such saintly forbearance as Shorthouse was displaying is rare in any singer, and in Shorthouse, Adam reflected, was positively unnatural. He was not altogether surprised, therefore, at the campaign of obstruction which coincided with the beginning of the orchestral rehearsals.

None the less, things went quite smoothly in the early stages, and up to the day of the murder only one incident occurred which it is necessary to relate. The protagonists were Shorthouse, Joan Davis, and a young girl named Judith Haynes.

It was a Monday evening. During the afternoon they had run straight through the last scene of act three, finishing at about six o'clock; and subsequently, Joan Davis remained in the rehearsal-room with Peacock to deal with various loose ends in her own part. Unknown to them, two other people were still in the theatre: Shorthouse, who was drinking heavily in his dressing-room (he had been by no means sober during the afternoon, though, as always, he sang magnificently), and Judith Haynes, a member of the chorus, who had stayed on with a view to altering her costume which fitted badly.

At seven Peacock left, and Joan went up to her dressing-room to fetch a coat and scarf. In the chorus dressing-room she found Shorthouse, exceedingly drunk, doing his best to remove the clothes from Judith Haynes, who was struggling inexpertly with him. Joan – by no means a puny or a nervous woman – acted with vigour and promptness. In falling, Shorthouse caught his head on the angle of the door, and this contributed a good deal to quietening him. In fact, he lay without moving.

'And that is that,' said Joan, gazing at his supine form with workmanlike pride. She turned to the girl, who was dealing, scarlet-faced, with buttons and shoulder-straps, Joan saw that she was slender, fair, and young. 'Are you all right, my dear?'

'Y-yes, thank-you,' Judith stammered. 'I – I don't know what I should have done if you hadn't come along. I – He's not –?'

'No, no,' Joan reassured her. 'Breathing stertorously and very much alive. You'd better go home, hadn't you?'

'Yes. I – I don't know how to thank you.' Judith hesitated, and then added with a rush: 'Please – please don't tell anyone about this, will you? I should hate anyone to know . . .'

Joan frowned slightly. 'If it weren't a bit too late to get a substitute, I should see to it that Edwin was kicked out of this production.'

'No, you mustn't.' Judith spoke with surprising vehemence. 'I should be so ashamed if people knew . . .'

Being above all a practical woman, Joan was momentarily puzzled. 'Ashamed? But you're not to blame, child. Why on earth –?'

'It's just – oh, I don't know. But please – *please* promise.' Joan shrugged her shoulders and smiled. 'Of course, if you want it that way. Where do you live? If it isn't too far, I'll walk home with you.'

'It's awfully kind, but you really needn't bother . . .'

'Nonsense,' said Joan. 'I should like to. It's half an hour yet before my dinner-time.'

Judith was recovering her self-possession slowly. 'What about' – she nodded towards Shorthouse – 'him?'

'We'll leave him,' said Joan cheerfully. 'Edwin is unfortunately one of those people who always recover from things . . . Have you got a coat? Then let's make a move.'

On the way to Judith's lodgings in Clarendon Street, Joan learned a little more about it. It appeared that Shorthouse had been making some kind of advances ever since rehearsals began, and that Judith, though repulsing these, had been too shy of his professional eminence to be actively rude to him. Moreover, there was a young man – also in the chorus – who had aspirations as a composer of opera, and Judith had thought that Shorthouse might be able to help or advise him.

'I'll advise him, my dear.' said Joan. 'And so will Adam, on pain of instant excommunication. But as to helping – well, virtually the only way to get a new opera put on is to be a multi-millionaire.'

She was very thoughtful as she walked back to the 'Mace and Sceptre'. Edwin Shorthouse plainly was heading for a shipwreck from which not even his voice and his artistry would save him. It was a pity, Joan thought, that she could not assist in propelling him on to the rocks by publicizing this evening's occurrence, but a promise was a promise. That she was obliged at least to break it was due to circumstances which few people could have foreseen.

Chapter Four

Presently the orchestral rehearsals began, and with them, trouble.

Adam sighed windily, took out a packet of Spearmint chewing-gum, and placed part of its contents slowly in his mouth. His gaze, roving over the auditorium, came to rest on John Barfield, who was slumped in one of the front stalls, gobbling a ham sandwich and dropping the crumbs down the front of his waistcoat. The rapid and rhythmical movement of his jaws was obscurely fascinating. Adam stared until Barfield looked up sharply and caught his eye; then turned, with some dignity, to reconsider what was going on on the stage.

Or rather, what was not going on. 'It is extraordinary,' thought Adam, 'that Edwin is able to find something wrong even when he's only sitting still, singing a monologue.' The cause of the present stoppage had eluded Adam in the first instance, but it appeared from the logomachy that was now in progress that it had something to do with tempo. 'Naturally I defer to you absolutely, Mr Peacock,' Shorthouse was saying without a hint of deference across the footlights. 'It's simply that I've not been used to such a marked accelerando at that point, and I felt that Sachs' dignity was rather lessened by it.'

George Peacock fidgeted with his baton and looked harassed. And well he might, Adam reflected: rehearsing *Die Meistersinger* with Edwin Shorthouse in the cast had unnerved many an older and more experienced conductor. It was really all a great pity; Peacock was an able young man; this production would certainly be important to his career; and after four weeks' nagging by Edwin Shorthouse he might easily make a mess of the actual show. Moreover – Adam glanced at his watch – time was getting on; they still had the third act to get through that afternoon.

'Why, in the name of God,' he whispered to Joan Davis, 'can't Edwin shut his trap for ten minutes at a time?'

Joan nodded briskly. 'Inelegantly put,' she returned, 'but I could scarcely agree with you more. I'm very sorry for that young man. It's just the greatest pity in the world that Edwin happens to be so good.'

'He wouldn't have lasted five minutes if he hadn't been,' said Adam. 'And I'm inclined to think that someone may stick a knife in him yet.'

'. . . So if you've got no objection,' Peacock was saying from the rostrum, 'we'll keep it as it was. I think the extra impetus is wanted at that point.'

'Of course,' said Shorthouse. 'Of course. I must try to follow your beat more closely. If I might have a more definite down-stroke at "springtime's behest"—'

'Ass,' Joan commented in a vehement whisper from the wings. 'Contemptible ass. The wretched man's beat is perfectly clear.'

'If we have many more hold-ups,' Adam replied gloomily, 'we shall never get on to the third act at all. Not that I should be altogether sorry,' he added as an afterthought. 'I tried to sing a top A in my bath this morning, and nothing but a sort of whistling sound came out.'

The music began again. Adam had heard it hundreds of times, but still it cast its warm enchantment over him. They reached the disputed passage. Shorthouse was dragging.

'Now we shall see,' said Joan.

Peacock tapped with his baton and the orchestra faded into silence. 'I'm afraid we were a little ahead of you. Mr Shorthouse,' he said pointedly.

'Oh, Lord,' groaned Adam. 'Not sarcasm. *Not* sarcasm, you fool.'

The result was as he expected. There was a moment's dead silence, and then: 'If my efforts displease you, Mr Peacock,' said Shorthouse, 'I would be obliged if you would tell me so in a straightforward way, and not by means of cheap witticisms.'

There was another silence. Peacock flushed scarlet. Then: 'I think we'll leave that passage for the moment,' he said quietly, 'and go on. We'll take it from scene four – Eva's entry. Are you ready, Miss Davis?' he called.

'Perfectly,' Joan called back. 'Even the pretence of flirting with Edwin,' she said to Adam, 'makes me shudder.'

'Never mind. Perhaps he'll object to something you do. Then you can give him hell.'

'How nice that would be,' said Joan dreamily. 'But there's not much hope of it. He only picks on the young and inexperienced, who can't answer back . . . Here we go.'

'Ta-ta,' said Adam. 'Meet you under the lime-tree, and don't bring a friend.' He returned to his reflexions.

The situation was, in fact, worrying. There could be no doubt that Peacock was breaking up under the strain of incessant objections, interruptions, and superfluous requests for information about tempo, dynamics, and all the paraphernalia which should have been, and in fact *had* been, settled at the piano rehearsals; doing a complex, five-hour opera is labour enough without any member of the cast's making a wilful nuisance of himself. What made it more objectionable was that where the opera management was concerned, Shorthouse could twist Peacock round his little finger, for Shorthouse was the box-office attraction, and Peacock virtually a nonentity; so that although *nominally* Peacock's word was law . . .

Adam sighed, took another piece of chewing-gum, and again caught the eye of Barfield, who was beginning to eat a tomato. Barfield grimaced and nodded meaningly at the stage. Adam grimaced back. It was a futile interchange. At the other side of the stage, Shorthouse and Joan chanted mellifluously at one another, while the orchestra tranquillized, with an occasional tender dissonance, in A flat. Adam noticed suddenly how exceptionally well they were playing, and his anger with Shorthouse rose afresh. To calm himself, he took a third piece of chewing-gum. It was a pity the stuff lost its taste so quickly, and became merely rubbery.

A few moments later he was joined by Dennis Rutherston, the producer, and a dark, rather ill-looking young man whom he vaguely remembered as being the apprentice whose sole duty it is, in the first act, to explain (in two words) the absence of Niklaus Vogel from the Masters' gathering.

'It's a trial,' said Rutherston, 'not being able to move people when they're singing. A convention, if you ask me.' He was a melancholy, youngish man who was never to be seen without a battered trilby hat on his head.

'It sends one out of tune,' Adam told him kindly.

'And what a nuisance Shorthouse is being . . . The meadow scene's going to be an unholy muddle,' Rutherston prognosticated gloomily. 'These damned apprentices *will not* stand still when they get to their places. They seem to imagine that if they shift about from foot to foot it produces an appearance of animation. Actually, it looks like a mass attack of incipient D.T.s.'

Beyond them, the music ceased abruptly. 'Hullo,' muttered Rutherston. 'What now?'

'It seems impossible to rehearse this work for five minutes' – Peacock's voice was shaking – 'without an obbligato of muffled altercation from the wings. Will you please be quiet!'

'That's *us*,' said Rutherston, faintly surprised. 'Well, anyway, I must be off.' As the music started again, he drifted away, followed by the dark young man.

'God help us all,' said Adam to himself, with some feeling. He had not liked the nerve-racked tone of Peacock's voice, which suggested an imminent explosion. And he knew from experience that if one person loses control of himself at a rehearsal, the rest always begin to sulk, and the only thing to do is to pack up and go home. He devoutly hoped that Shorthouse would keep quiet for a while.

Magdalena trotted to the stage and held her brief colloquy with Eva. It occurred to Adam that he had better get upstage in readiness for his entry, and he affixed his chewing-gum providently to a piece of scenery. Damn Shorthouse, he thought, as he passed Beckmesser twanging faintly at his lute; damn the man.

In another moment Joan was rushing to greet him. 'Hero, poet, and my only friend!' she sang, embracing him, and added under her breath: 'You smell revoltingly of peppermint.'

Very much to Adam's surprise, the rest of the second act passed without untoward incident. The lovers attempted to elope and were foiled by Sachs: Beckmesser performed his ludicrous serenade and was chased by David amid a rout of apprentices and masters ('Looks like a lot of fairies,' said Rutherston with disapproval, 'dancing a ballet'); sleepy-eyed, the night-watchman came on, intoned his formula, blew his horn; and to echoes of the summer-night motif and of Beckmesser's serenade the music came to an end. But Adam suspected that Shorthouse, whose tactics in nuisance were subtle, was merely holding his fire until the third act: and events proved him to be right.

The cast gathered on the stage to hear the respective strictures of conductor, producer, and chorus-master. There followed a quarter-hour break, in which people drifted out to get a cup of tea. Adam joined Joan Davis and Barfield, who was eating an apple, in the stalls.

'There are times,' he said, 'when I really think we ought to get together and raise Hades about Shorthouse.'

'Calm before the storm,' said Barfield indistinctly. 'That's all this is. But if you ask me, the management wouldn't take it kindly.'

'For the simple reason,' Joan put in, 'that they don't realize what a marvel Peacock is with the orchestra. He makes that cynical old gang of scrapers and blowers sound positively beautiful.'

'It's youth,' Barfield mumbled through his apple. 'Emotional osmosis.'

'Where is he, by the way?' Adam asked. 'Has he gone out?'

He stared about him. On the stage a number of unlikely objects which had been temporarily employed to represent a Nuremberg street were now being shifted about to represent a meadow. In his gallery at the back, the electrician was conversing with a couple of apprentices. And several members of the chorus were wandering dispiritedly up and down the gangways of the auditorium. But of Peacock there was no sign.

'Having a heart-to-heart with Shorthouse, perhaps,' suggested Barfield. 'Poor devil.' He took out a piece of cake and offered it perfunctorily to Adam and Joan; he was obviously relieved when they refused.

The dark young man whom Adam had seen with the producer crossed the back of the stage, talking to Judith Haynes. 'Who's that?' Adam enquired generally.

'The man?' Joan sat up to get a better look. 'Oh, Boris somebody. One of the apprentices.'

'Isn't the girl something to do with Shorthouse?'

'As to that,' said Joan rather definitely, 'I couldn't say. If so, I'm sorry for her. She's a pretty child.'

'Chorus?'

'Yes. One of the boatload of maidens. It's she who dances with David.'

'Oh, yes, so it is.' Adam considered. 'I felt sure I'd seen her with Shorthouse, but she looks very much attached to that young man.'

'Promiscuous probably,' said Barfield, dropping cake-crumbs on to his knee. 'Are we doing scene one of the last act? If so, I've time to go out and get a bite to eat.'

Joan shook her head. 'No, only the second scene. Just as well, too. Everyone's a bit worn.'

Barfield was staring at the door leading backstage, which now opened. 'Cripes,' he said. 'Here's Mephisto. Turn on the charm, everyone.'

Shorthouse came up to them, sat down, and heaved a sigh. He smelled, as usual, of gin.

'Thank God the show's in a week,' he said. 'I can't stand

much more of this. Peacock's all right,' – he spoke with such manifest insincerity that Adam started – 'but he can't make up his mind about anything.'

Joan said: 'Are you deliberately trying to harry him into a nervous breakdown, Edwin?'

'Good heavens, Joan' – Shorthouse looked genuinely shocked – 'what's put that idea into your head? I'm sorry if I've been holding the production up, but I must understand what I'm supposed to be doing. Yet every time I ask, I get some kind of vulgar insult hurled at me . . . Not that I mind, personally – the man's inexperienced and he's obviously nervous. But I'm worried about the production as a whole. This is the first time *Meistersinger*'s been done since before the war, and it seems to me that for that reason it's more than ordinarily important to get everything exactly right.' He paused, and involuntarily a smile flitted across his face. 'I've been considering going to the management and asking them to replace Peacock.'

'Don't be such a damned fool,' said Adam, more sharply than he had intended. 'He's under contract.'

'So am I,' Shorthouse countered unpleasantly. 'But that's not going to stop me walking out if rehearsals continue on the present lines. I can assure you it isn't a personal matter: it's only Wagner I'm thinking of.'

The notion that Shorthouse might be thinking of anyone but himself was almost too much for Adam; he uttered an incoherent snorting sound. Barfield was unwinding a packet of chocolate. Pogner strode across the stage, muttering fiercely to himself, and Rutherston appeared, gesticulating at the electrician in his gallery. A horn-player in the orchestra pit was engaged in a prolonged Jeremiad about some infraction of Union rules.

Ten minutes later the rehearsal was under way again. The Guilds entered; the boatload of maidens arrived; the apprentices danced ('like a Sunday School treat,' Rutherston remarked); and last of all came the Mastersingers, headed by a banner bearing an effigy of David and his harp. The chorus sang in honour of Sachs; as the acclamation died away, all was ready for the moving response of the cobbler-poet.

Chapter Five

And that was when the real trouble started.

There was a minor hitch over positioning, followed by a misunderstanding as to the point in the score at which the music was to be recommenced. Shorthouse snapped at Peacock; Peacock snapped back at him, and then they went for one another, as Adam afterwards put it, 'like a nationalization debate in the Commons'. Although it was an eruption which everyone had expected, the embarrassment was general, since the sight of two grown-up men bawling at one another like children is at the best of times dispiriting. No one, however, interfered; only, when Peacock finally stalked out, after smashing his baton on the conductor's desk in an access of blind fury, Adam went quietly after him. He heard the murmur of released tension as he left the stage.

Peacock was in the rehearsal-room. He stood quite still, gripping the lid of the piano with both hands and struggling to control his emotions. His bony, irregular, sensitive features betrayed the strain he was undergoing, and his eyes were momentarily vacant and unseeing. Adam hesitated for an instant in the doorway; then said briefly:

'You have my sympathy.'

There was a considerable pause before Peacock replied. At last he relaxed and said with great bitterness:

'I suppose I should apologize.'

'Technically, yes,' Adam commented. 'Humanly, no. You must realize that everyone is on your side. Edwin is behaving intolerably.'

Peacock muttered.

'I ought to be able to control a situation like that. After all, it's all part of my job . . .' He considered. 'You've more experience of these things than I . . . Should I resign?'

'Don't be a fool,' said Adam warmly. 'Of course not.'

'Naturally, I realize' – Peacock spoke with difficulty – 'the line it's desirable to take. Genial but firm . . . The trouble is, my nerves won't let me do it. I suppose really I'm unfitted for this kind of work.' He looked so haggard that Adam was shocked. 'But I've simply *got* to make a success of it. One way or another, it's going to affect the whole of my future career.'

There was a silence. 'What about the rehearsal?' Adam asked.

'Tell them it's over, will you? I can't face people at present.'

'It would be better if you—'

'For God's sake tell them it's over!'

Peacock checked himself abruptly, and a spasm of shame passed over his face. 'I'm sorry. I didn't mean to shout.'

'I'll tell them,' said Adam, and hesitated.

'For the love of heaven don't do anything rash,' he added, and returned to the stage.

There he made his brief announcement. Shorthouse, he observed, was not present to hear it.

People drifted away, chattering in a subdued fashion. The orchestra began to dismantle and pack up their instruments. Joan Davis accosted Adam.

'How is he?' she asked.

'I don't like it,' said Adam. 'I don't like it at all. Where's Edwin?'

'He left immediately after Peacock.'

Adam sighed. 'Well, there's no point in lingering here. Let's go back to the hotel and get a drink.'

'Do you think we should have a conference?'

'A conference . . . I scarcely see what would come of it.'

Joan smiled wryly. 'Nothing, in all probability. But it might clear the air.'

'After dinner, then – preferably over a drink.'

'I'll arrange something.' Joan nodded briskly, and went off to her dressing-room.

At the stage door Adam met Shorthouse on the point of leaving.

On a sudden impulse: 'What the hell is the matter with you, Edwin?' he demanded.

Shorthouse looked at him queerly, almost blankly. His thin grey hair was dishevelled, and there was sweat on his cheeks and forehead. It came to Adam, with a sudden twinge of horror, that the man might be growing insane. Irrationally, and quite unexpectedly, Adam had a feeling of pity.

But it was wiped away when Shorthouse spoke – thickly, as though the movement of his mouth were painful to him.

'I shall telephone Levi,' he said, 'and get that little whippersnapper kicked out.'

'Don't be a fool, Edwin.' Adam spoke sharply. 'Even if Levi agreed, it'd be the beginning of the end for you. You can't antagonize people beyond a certain point without suffering for it.'

But Shorthouse, surprisingly, took no offence. 'Suffering,' he repeated dully. 'People don't realize how *I* suffer already . . .'

He paused: then, collecting himself, blundered out into the early darkness.

Adam followed him shortly afterwards.

Dennis Rutherston, the inevitable hat perched on the back of his head, leaned back and stared fixedly at the pale amber of the whisky in his glass.

'Why worry?' he said. 'It'll smooth itself out. These things always do.'

'I'm sorry,' Adam interposed with unwonted vigour. 'But I don't agree.'

They were in the bar of the Randolph Hotel, seated round a table near the door – Adam, Elizabeth, Joan, Rutherston, Karl Wolzogen, and John Barfield. It was eight o'clock of the same evening, and the after-dinner crowd had not yet collected. Nonetheless, a few persistent drinkers shared the room with them. At a neighbouring table, a tall, dark man with a green scarf round his neck was holding forth learnedly on the subject of rat-poisons to a neat middle-aged gentleman of military aspect and an auburn-haired youth with unsteady hands and a rose in his buttonhole. The place was predominantly blue and cream. It was blessedly warm after the cold outside. The clink of glasses, the angry fizzing of a beer-machine behind the bar, and the bell of the cash-register mingled agreeably with the hum of conversation.

Adam was argumentative. 'This thing is cumulative,' he stated, wagging his forefinger at them by way of warning. 'It isn't sporadic. And in Edwin's case it seems to be compli- cated by self-pity. But what it amounts to in the end is this: that either Edwin or Peacock will have to go if we're to open at all.'

Edmund Crispin

'. . . red squill,' said the dark man at the next table. 'It causes a very painful death.'

Rutherston sighed. 'Well, what do you suggest?' he asked. 'A deputation to Levi?'

'We've been over all this ground already.' Joan Davis, whom the events of the afternoon had made a trifle reckless in the matter of smoking, lit a new cigarette from the end of the old. 'Levi would never agree to getting rid of Edwin. Edwin's still box-office, remember. No operatic management can afford to annoy him.'

'Well, for that matter,' said Adam irritably, 'no operatic management can afford to annoy us.'

'Dear Adam.' Joan patted his hand affectionately. 'Are you suggesting that we threaten to walk out if Edwin isn't removed? Because I, for one, don't feel much like dealing with an action for breach of contract.'

There was a silence, which was broken at last by Karl Wolzogen.

'Ach!' he snorted. 'That fool! Art means nothing to him. The *Meister* means nothing to him. At the age of four I was presented to the *Meister*, in Bayreuth. It was the year before his death. He was abstracted, but kind, and he said—'

The others, though sympathizing with Karl's enthusiasm for this elevating, if precocious experience, had all of them heard about it several times before. They hastened to bring the conversation back to the problem of Shorthouse.

'Well, have *you* any views, John?' Joan demanded.

Barfield, who was eating ginger biscuits from a paper bag on the table in front of him, choked noisily as a crumb lodged in his windpipe.

'It seems to me that there's only one answer,' he announced when he had recovered. 'And that is—'

'Zinc phosphide,' said the dark man at the next table. 'A singularly effective poison.'

Barfield was momentarily unnerved by the appositeness of this.

'I was going to say,' he proceeded cautiously, 'that we shall simply have to let Peacock go.'

There were cries of protest.

'All right, all right!' he added hastily. 'I know it's unjust. I know it's detestable. I know the heavens will cry aloud for vengeance. But what other solution *is* there?'

'Zinc phosphide,' Elizabeth suggested. It was her first contribution to the discussion.

'It would be nice,' said Joan wistfully, 'if we could poison him just a little – just so as to make him unable to sing.'

And perhaps it was at this point that the conference drifted away from the subject of Shorthouse. Certainly it had become apparent by then that no fresh light on the matter was forthcoming. At about nine the party broke up, and Adam walked back to the 'Mace and Sceptre' with Elizabeth and Joan.

It was after eleven when he discovered that his pocket-book was missing. Elizabeth was already in bed, and Adam was undressing. The process of disburdening his pockets revealed the loss, and he remembered that during the evening he had paid for drinks out of an accumulation of change.

'Damn!' he said, irresolute. 'I believe I left it in my dressing-room at the theatre. I really think I'd better go and fetch it.'

'Won't tomorrow do?' said Elizabeth. Adam thought that she looked particularly beautiful tonight, with her hair glowing like satin in the light of the bedside lamp.

He shook his head. 'I really shan't feel happy unless I go and get it. There's rather a lot of money in it.'

Edmund Crispin

'But won't the theatre be locked up?'

'Well, it may be. But the old stage door keeper sleeps there, and he may not have gone to bed yet. I'll try, anyway.' He was dressing again as he spoke.

'All right, darling.' Elizabeth's voice was sleepy. 'Don't be long.'

Adam went over and kissed her. 'I won't,' he promised. 'It's only three minutes' walk.'

When he got outside, he found that the moon was gibbous, very pale, and with a halo encircling it. Its light illuminated the whole of the south side of George Street, and at the end, at the junction with Cornmarket, he could see the steady green of the traffic signals. A belated cyclist pedalled past, his tyres crackling on the ice which flecked the surface of the road. Adam's breath steamed in the cold air; but at least the wind had dropped.

He crossed Gloucester Green. There were still a few cars parked there, the pale moonlight on their metal roofs striped with the yellower rays of the street-lamps. It was very quiet, save for the persistent coughing of a belated wayfarer stationed ouside the little tobacconist's shop on his left. Adam paused for a moment to read the concert announcements posted on a nearby wall, and then walked on into Beaumont Street.

He had no difficulty in entering the opera-house – indeed, the stage door stood wide open, though the little foyer inside, with its green baize notice-board and its single frosted bulb, was deserted. By about twenty-five past eleven he had retrieved his pocket-book and was preparing to depart.

His dressing-room was on the first floor, and his decision to go down in the lift must therefore be ascribed solely to enjoyment of the motion. He pressed the button, and the apparatus descended. He climbed in, and traversed the short distance to the ground floor. Then, feeling this short journey to be inadequate, he ascended again, this time to the second floor. Through the iron gates he could see the long, gloomy corridor of dressing-rooms, the gleam of the telephone fixed to the wall at the far end, and the rectangle of yellow light which came from the open door of the stage door keeper's bedroom. After a moment, the stage door keeper himself shuffled out of it. He was an old man named Furbelow, with wispy hair and steel-rimmed spectacles. Adam, sensing perhaps that his presence required some explanation, opened the lift gates and greeted him.

'Ah, sir,' said the old man with some relief. 'It's you.'

Adam accounted dutifully for his late visit. 'But I'm surprised,' he added, 'to find you still up.'

'I'm always up till midnight, Mr Langley, and I keep the stage door open till then. But it's cold down below, so I comes and sits up 'ere during the last part o' the evening.'

'I should have thought it was equally cold up here, if you keep the door of your room open.'

'I as to do that, sir, when the electric fire's on. Them things exude gases,' said Furbelow a shade didactically. 'You 'ave to 'ave ventilation when they're alight.'

Adam, though doubting if there was much basis for this assertion, was not sufficiently interested in the stage door keeper's domestic affairs to argue about it. He said goodnight and left the theatre. As he was walking away, a car drew up, and its occupant, a man, hurriedly entered the stage door. Adam experienced a mild curiosity, but he did not linger, and by the time he had arrived back at the hotel the incident was forgotten.

Meanwhile, in a dressing-room almost directly opposite

to Furbelow's open door, Edwin Shorthouse swayed a little in a cold draught. Now and again the rope creaked against the iron hook from which he was suspended, but that was the only sound.

Chapter Six

'It argues a certain poverty of imagination,' said Gervase Fen with profound disgust, 'that in a world where atom physicists walk the streets unharmed, emitting their habitual wails about the misuse of science by politicians, a murderer can find a no more deserving victim than some unfortunate opera singer . . .'

'You'd scarcely say that,' Adam answered, 'if you'd known Shorthouse. He will not be very much mourned.'

The three men paused on the kerb to let a lorry go by before crossing St Giles'. A little whirlwind of snow-flakes was swept among them by the wind.

'All the same,' Fen resumed when they were half-way across, 'good singers are rare. And as far as I'm able to judge' – his confident manner tended to nullify this reservation – 'he *was* good.'

'Certainly he was good. No one would have put up with him for two minutes if he hadn't been . . . Is the snow going to lie, one wonders?'

'It seems to me you're overhasty in assuming it was murder,' said Sir Richard Freeman, the Chief Constable of Oxford. He walked very upright, with short, rapid, determined steps. 'Mudge implied that the circumstances suggested suicide.' He frowned severely at this Jamesian hyperbole.

'*Mudge*,' Fen remarked with emotion. He buffeted his arms across his chest in the manner associated with taxi-drivers. 'That hurts,' he complained. 'Anyway, if it was suicide, I scarcely see how it's likely to interest me.'

'Shorthouse. Any relation of the composer?'

'Charles Shorthouse?' said Adam. 'Yes. A brother. Edwin sang in a good many of Charles' operas, though as far as the normal repertory was concerned he specialized in Wagner. Wotan and Sachs. Mark. That chatterbox Gurnemanz. He was the obvious Sachs when they decided to put on *Meistersinger* here.'

They passed a public-house. 'I should like a Burton,' said Fen, gazing back at it with the lugubrious passion of Orpheus surveying Eurydice at hell-mouth. 'But I suppose it's too early. Shorthouse was hanged, wasn't he?'

'So it appears.' Sir Richard Freeman nodded. 'But not strangled. It seems to have been a kind of judicial hanging.'

'You mean his neck was broken?'

'Or dislocated. We shall get the full medical report when we arrive.'

'It's by no means a common way to commit suicide,' Fen commented. His normally cheerful, ruddy face was thoughtful. 'In fact, the arranging of it would involve a certain amount of knowledge and finesse.' He buttoned at the neck the enormous raincoat in which he was muffled, and adjusted his extraordinary hat. He was forty-three years old, lean, lanky, with blue eyes and brown hair ineffectually plastered down with water. 'I gather,' he pursued as they turned up Beaumont Street by the Randolph Hotel, 'that Shorthouse had been causing trouble at rehearsals.'

'Trouble,' said Adam grimly, 'is an understatement. By the way' – he turned to the Chief Constable – 'I asked my wife along to the theatre this morning. I hope you don't mind. You see, it's rather in her line.'

'Your *wife*,' said Sir Richard, heavily, like one burdened suddenly with a dangerous secret. 'I didn't know you were married, Langley.'

'Adam's wife,' Fen explained, 'is Elizabeth Harding, who writes books about crime.'

'Ah,' said Sir Richard. 'Nasty subject,' he added rather offensively. 'Yes, of course. By all means. Delighted to meet her.'

'I rather think she wants to interview you, Gervase,' Adam continued. 'She's doing a series on famous detectives for one of the papers.'

'*Famous detectives*,' said Fen with great complacency. 'Oh, my dear paws. You hear that, Dick?' he went on, banging the Chief Constable suddenly on the chest to make sure of his attention. '*Famous detectives*.'

'Celebrated imbeciles,' said Sir Richard crossly. 'Ugh.'

'Anyway,' Adam put in, 'here we are.'

Crossing the entrance to St John Street, they arrived at the opera-house, and made their way, Fen grumbling in quite a distressing way about the cold, to the stage door, which they found guarded by a constable. Nearby, a small group of seedy-looking men with instrument cases, their coat collars turned up against the biting wind and their fingers blue and numb, were conversing with a female harpist.

'Morning, Mr Langley,' said one of them. 'Queer business, isn't it? Shall we be getting a rehearsal, do you imagine?'

'Not until the afternoon, anyway,' Adam returned. 'It depends on the police, I should say.'

'They won't cancel the production, will they?'

'No surely not. We'll get a new Sachs. But it'll probably mean postponing the first show.'

'Well, I'm for the boozer,' said the oboist. 'Coming, anyone?'

The constable saluted Sir Richard Freeman. He saluted Fen, more dubiously. He did not salute Adam at all. They went inside.

The stage door led into a small stone vestibule, from which flights of stairs ran up and down. There was a kind of cavity, furnished with a few elementary comforts, where in the daytime the stage door keeper lived, moved, and had his being, but this was at present empty. They pushed through a padded swing-door into the wings. Semi-darkness greeted them. Moving cautiously among ropes, floodlamps, and scenery poised precariously against the walls, they came within earshot, and soon within sight, of some kind of altercation which was in progress on the stage.

Beneath a single working lamp, high up among the battens, stood Elizabeth and an Inspector of police, both of them very angry indeed. Dimly in the background there were other forms hovering, like wraiths on the threshold of limbo, but these two appeared to be the centre of such activity as was going forward at the moment. The Inspector of police was small, wizened, and malevolent in appearance; and Elizabeth was standing with her hands on her hips, glowering at him.

'You are an intolerable, pompous ass,' she was informing him in measured, judicial tones. 'A jack-in-office. A nincompoop. A giddy-brained pigeon.'

'Listen to me,' said the Inspector with theatrical restraint. 'Just you listen to me. I've had quite enough of you. You've no right to be here, young woman. And if you don't get out – now: *instantly* – I shall charge you with obstructing me in the performance of my duties.'

'I'd like to see you try,' Elizabeth replied, in a voice of such intense malignancy that even Fen was startled. She swung round to face the newcomers. 'And if you think—' She broke off, and her face suddenly brightened. 'Adam!'

'Darling, are you being a nuisance?' Adam asked. 'I want you to meet Sir Richard Freeman, the Chief Constable, and Gervase Fen. Elizabeth, my wife.'

'Pleasure,' said Sir Richard with manly gruffness. 'It's all right, Mudge,' he added to the enraged Inspector.

'As you say, sir,' Mudge answered. 'As you say, of course. As you say.' He stood back, muttering waspishly.

'Well, well.' Fen beamed at Elizabeth like an ogre about to gobble up a small boy. 'I *am* pleased. I could tell you some things about Adam,' he went on with great amiability.

'You've only rescued me just in time.' Elizabeth's voice still held a trace of peevishness. 'Adam darling, you're terribly late.'

'Yes, dear,' said Adam soothingly. 'I'm sorry.'

'Now,' said Sir Richard, who was plainly not much interested by this interchange, 'let's have a few facts, Mudge. Is this where it happened?'

He gazed about him. The light from the stage faintly illuminated the front rows of the stalls. Half-painted flats projected from the wings. Backstage, the electrician's gallery was visible. There was a lot of litter and a lot of dust. There were half-effaced chalk marks scrawled on the floor by the producer, to assist positioning at rehearsals. In the orchestra-pit, a tangle of brass stands could be seen. But there was nothing, apart from a good deal of rope, to suggest suicide or violence.

'No, sir,' Mudge informed his superior with perhaps more testiness than was altogether wise. 'Not here. In the dressing-room.'

'Well, take us there, then,' said Sir Richard. 'It's absurd to stand about like a set of characters in a melodrama.'

Mudge sighed, and pronounced, as though it were a rune, the word 'Furbelow'. The stage door keeper materialized from among the peripheral wraiths, and stood blinking at them. 'Good morning, Mr Langley,' he said uncertainly.

'Furbelow, you'd better come with us.' Mudge was peremptory. 'Sir Richard will want to hear what you have to say.'

'Who's this?' Sir Richard demanded with distaste.

'The stage door keeper, sir. His evidence is important.'

'Indeed?' said Sir Richard, like one confronted too suddenly with a freak of nature. 'Important. I see.'

'Come on, come on,' said Fen impatiently. 'Or we shall never get started.'

They made their way off the stage. Adam wanted to take the lift, but it appeared that the aspen and decrepit Furbelow went in fear of lifts. The machinery broke, he explained, and one was precipitated with violence to the ground . . . In any case, this particular lift was too small to take all of them, so they walked up, encouraged by some remarks from the Chief Constable on the subject of muscular development – the Inspector first, Sir Richard following, Fen at his heels, then Adam and Elizabeth, and finally Furbelow. Having arrived at the second floor, they made their way in single file round an inconveniently placed iron ladder which led to the roof, and at last came to a door bearing a card with the inscription EDWIN SHORTHOUSE on it. The Inspector halted.

'It's here,' he said.

'Well, *well*,' said Sir Richard, annoyed at the redundancy of this statement. 'Let's have a look at it. The – ah – he's been moved, I suppose?'

'Oh, yes, sir.' Mudge was inserting a key into the lock. 'In fact the post mortem ought to be over by now. I'm expecting Rashmole back here at any time.'

'Have you got in touch with the brother?'

Mudge paused in his labours, to everyone's great annoyance; the corridor was undeniably draughty. 'I wired him earlier this morning, sir,' he said. 'And the reply came a few minutes before you arrived just now.' He hesitated. 'Rather an odd reply. Unnatural, to my thinking.'

'Well, what was it?'

Mudge abandoned the door and groped in his pockets; a telegram was produced; they passed it from hand to hand; it ran:

DELIGHTED HOPING FOR THIS FOR MONTHS SUICIDE EH QUERY DONT BOTHER ME NOW CHARLES SHORTHOUSE.

'Well, I'm damned.' Sir Richard was indignant. 'This thing must be a practical joke.'

'I scarcely think so,' said Adam. 'Charles Shorthouse is a very eccentric person, you know. And notoriously he loathed his brother. It strikes me as being exactly the kind of wire he would send.'

'Where does he live, anyway?'

'Near Amersham, I believe.'

'Very well . . . Mudge, will you please open that door?'

They got inside at last. It was a large dressing-room – like all dressing-rooms untidy, and like all dressing-rooms dirty. Clothes suspended haphazardly from hooks, or lay in heaps on the chairs. The dressing-table was a litter of grease-paints and photographs. A vocal score of *Die Meistersinger*, tattered and scrawled upon, lay on the floor. There were one or two books, lightly coated with powder; two empty beer bottles, and one half-full; a wash-basin; a typewriter; some blank sheets of paper. Windows were lacking, so they switched on the frosted bulbs which projected on either side of the mirror; but in one part of the room, where the ceiling was indented, there was a small skylight about three inches square, which could be opened from the roof.

'He seems to have made himself at home,' Fen commented. 'Dress rehearsals haven't started yet, have they?'

'No. But he always spent a good deal of time in his dressing-room,' said Adam. 'Drinking, mostly. There ought to be a bottle or two of gin somewhere about. He was very addicted to it.'

'There was,' said Mudge. 'And it's being analysed at this moment. Here' – Adam was momentarily overwhelmed by the illusion of being on a conducted tour – 'here is where the body hung. Hang,' Mudge added uncertainly.

'Hung,' said Fen kindly. 'Dear me. It hardly looks as if there'd be sufficient drop for him to break his neck.'

'In the execution shed,' Elizabeth put in briskly, 'they allow from six to eight feet, according to weight.'

Fen regarded her warily. 'Yes,' he admitted. 'You're quite right. But of course, it's all a matter of tensions. With luck – I don't quite know why I should say luck – you might break your neck dropping just a foot or so.'

They gazed at the stout iron hook from which the rope had hung. It was embedded in the ceiling about a foot from the indentation which contained the skylight, and about seven feet from the skylight itself.

'What's it there for?' asked Sir Richard, getting out his pipe. 'Was it there before?'

Furbelow, consulted by Mudge, opined that it had not been there before.

'And moreover,' said Mudge, 'there's flakes of plaster on the floor. Evidently a recent job, put there for the purpose . . . Well, he was hanging from that. There was nothing special about the rope – just a length of ordinary clothes-line—'

'Was there a knot,' Fen inquired, 'under the angle of the jaw?' He had sat down, and was fingering his own jaw, meditatively.

'Why, yes, sir, there was. Whether it was him or someone else that was responsible, they evidently knew what they were about.' Mudge paused, contemplating retrospectively, Adam fancied, the grammar of this sentence.

Sir Richard struck a match. 'Go on,' he said, waving it encouragingly. It went out.

'The inside of the rope was padded' – Mudge had fallen into a kind of sing-song which evidently he considered suitable to his recital – 'with some old cotton stuff. And – well, that's really all, I suppose.'

'*All?*' exclaimed Sir Richard. 'Don't be ridiculous, Mudge. It can't be *all*. Who found the body? And when?'

'It was found,' Mudge announced, 'by Dr Shand.'

'Shand?' Fen had been standing in front of the mirror, painting a large black moustache on his face. He now turned and exhibited the result. Elizabeth uttered a little squeal of delight. Fen frowned at her. 'Shand's a reliable man, Dick,' he continued. 'But what was he doing here in the middle of the night?'

'For the Lord's sake, Gervase,' said Sir Richard, 'stop playing with the grease-paint . . . Yes, Mudge.' He turned to the Inspector. 'What *was* he doing here in the middle of the night?'

'He came here,' Mudge explained hurriedly, 'in response to an urgent message from Shorthouse.'

'Ah. You say "message from". Who was responsible for the message?'

'That's just it. He doesn't know. It was a phone message.'

'This becomes interesting,' said Fen. He had applied removing-cream to his upper lip, and now looked as if he had been eating blancmange. 'So Shand turned up here. When, by the by?'

'About eleven-thirty. He came straight up here – up to the corridor outside, that is – and found Furbelow sitting in his bedroom opposite.'

'But look here,' said Adam suddenly, 'I was in the theatre last night.'

'Oh, Adam, so you were,' said Elizabeth in frank admiration.

'Good heavens, Adam, what were you doing?' Fen asked.

'I was fetching my notecase. I left it in my dressing-room during the afternoon rehearsal, and then forgot it. There was a lot of money in it, and things tend to disappear from dressing-rooms, so I came back for it as soon as I remembered. I must say, I never dreamed Edwin Shorthouse was here at all, let alone dead. What an appalling thing.'

Mudge appeared to be suffering from some obscure emotional upheaval. 'Now, sir,' he began, glancing uneasily at the Chief Constable, 'I'm afraid I haven't quite grasped who you are—'

'This is Adam Langley,' Fen said indistinctly through a towel, 'who's singing the part of Walther in *Die Meistersinger*.'

'The only first-rate tenor of reasonable girth,' Elizabeth added proudly, 'in Europe.'

'You fetched your notecase, sir. Very well. What time would this be?'

'Oh . . . twenty or twenty-five past eleven, I should say.'

'And your dressing-room is—?'

'On the floor below this.'

'Quite.' Mudge nodded sagaciously. 'Now, did you do anything else while you were in the theatre?'

'I went for a ride' – Adam spoke a little doubtfully – 'in the lift.'

'I beg your pardon, sir?'

'I went for a ride in the lift,' Adam repeated more firmly. 'I like lifts. They give me a queer feeling inside.'

'I should have thought that for that very reason—'

'A *pleasant* feeling, of course.' Adam explained what he had done. 'I talked to Furbelow,' he concluded, and added irrelevantly: 'Apparently he sits all evening with his door open because of the gases which are exuded by electric fires.'

'Nonsense,' said Sir Richard with incisive common sense.

'Did you meet anyone other than Furbelow during your visit here?' Mudge demanded.

'No one. When I'd had my joy-ride, I went straight home . . . Oh, there's one thing, though. As I was leaving, I did see a car draw up outside the stage door. But I dare say that would have been the doctor.'

Fen did not appear greatly interested by these haphazard recollections. 'Well, that's enough of that,' he said brusquely. 'Let's get back to Shand's arrival, and the discovery of the body.'

Mudge coughed, and adopted an attitude suggestive of the elocution-school. 'Dr Shand opened the door' – he paused impressively – 'and saw Shorthouse hanging from the spot which I indicated.' He indicated it again. 'He immediately called to Furbelow, who as we know was in his bedroom opposite, and together they got the unfortunate gentleman down.

'Now here is the point.' Mudge shook his index finger at them, admonishing, it seemed, their inattentiveness. 'At this time Shorthouse was technically speaking still alive. That's to say that although breathing had stopped, his heart was still beating. I'm told that on occasions this happens in cases of judicial hanging. Dr Shand cut' – the Inspector consulted some kind of mental tablature – 'a radial artery, and circulation was still going on. Of course it was impossible to revive the man – the heart stopped only a few moments after he'd been got down. And I understand that this business of the heart beating after death can only last for a very few minutes – *at most.*'

No one spoke. Sir Richard was applying a match to his pipe, the light of it flickering fitfully over his brown, lined face, with its iron-grey hair and moustache. Fen had stopped fidgeting, and was sitting on the edge of the dressing-table, his pale blue eyes intent, his usual fantastic naivety for the moment in abeyance. Elizabeth was seated, with Adam leaning on the back of her chair. Furbelow, near the doorway, shifted from one foot to the other. And in the midst of them stood the Inspector, like a minor devil enumerating the canons of hell to a coven of particularly obtuse witches.

'So far, so good,' he went on. 'And I'd ask you to notice that there was no one in here apart from Shorthouse when Dr Shand arrived. Being a sensible man, he took the precaution of making sure of this, but you can see for yourself that there isn't a hiding-place anywhere. Moreover, there's literally no way in or out except by the door.'

Chapter Seven

Mudge sighed. 'We now come,' he said with obvious reluctance, 'to Furbelow. It's on his evidence, so far as I can see, that the verdict for suicide must depend.* Furbelow came up to his bedroom at a quarter to eleven. He settled down, as was his habit, with the door open.'

'It's the gases,' said Furbelow, eyeing Sir Richard defensively.

Mudge ignored this. 'At five to eleven,' he went on, 'a certain individual arrived and, after knocking, entered this dressing-room. As far as we know at present, that individual was the last person to see Mr Shorthouse alive.'

'Who was it?' Sir Richard demanded.

'His identity we haven't yet discovered.' Mudge was apologetic. 'Perhaps Mr Langley can help us there. A young man, as I gather, and a member of the chorus.'

'Dark he was,' Furbelow supplied. 'Dark and foreign looking.'

'Oh, I think I know who you mean,' said Adam. 'He's one of the apprentices. Boris somebody.'

---

* The reader may like to know, at this point, that Furbelow's evidence was in fact correct in every particular.

'You can't remember the surname, sir?'

'I'm afraid not. But I can point him out to you as soon as we get another rehearsal – or for that matter Furbelow can.'

'Very good, sir.' Mudge nodded his satisfaction. 'As you'll find in a moment, it isn't as urgently important as it might at first seem . . . This young man, then, was in here for about ten minutes, and—'

'Just one moment,' Fen interrupted. He turned to Furbelow. 'Did you hear them talking?'

'No, I didn't,' said Furbelow. 'But then, likely I wouldn't 'ave. These doors is thick.'

Mudge continued his narrative. 'When the young man at last emerged from this room, at about five past eleven, Furbelow – ah – accosted him.'

'I'm sorry,' said Fen, 'but I must interrupt again . . . Furbelow, when the door of this dressing-room is open, can you see *into* it from your room?'

'No sir. It's at a bit of an angle, like. I can just catch a glimpse of one corner, that's all.'

'I see . . . Go ahead, Inspector.'

'Furbelow,' said Mudge, 'accompanied the young man down to the stage door and said goodnight. He then immediately returned to his bedroom, and, looking at the clock on the mantelpiece saw that the time was ten minutes past eleven. He calculates that he can't have been away for more than three minutes at the most.'

'That's right,' said Furbelow admiringly. It was evident that he regarded this account as a marvel of accurate recollection.

'Finally,' Mudge announced climactically, 'he's prepared to swear that no one entered or left this room from ten minutes past eleven until the arrival of Dr Shand at half-past.'

'Did he watch the door,' Fen asked, 'while he was talking to Adam?'

'I 'ad it in the corner of me eye,' said Furbelow.

'Anyway,' Adam interposed, '*I* can vouch for that half-minute or so. I should certainly have seen if anyone had gone in or come out – there was plenty of light from the door of Furbelow's room.'

A faint but unmistakable expression of pleasure appeared on Fen's ruddy countenance. 'Two questions, Inspector,' he said. 'First: was there a chair, or anything, from which Shorthouse could have jumped, if he committed suicide?'

'Yes, sir. One of those tall stools they put in front of bars, so you can never get a drink for the people sitting on them. According to Furbelow, it came from the property room. It's been taken away to be tested for foot-marks and fingerprints. It was lying on its side just by the body.'

'Yes. And while we're on the subject of fingerprints, was there anything on that hook in the ceiling?'

'Nothing you could identify. Just a few smudges.'

'I see. Furbelow, did you hear a bump at any stage, such as might have been caused by the stool falling over?'

'I did, sir.' Furbelow was markedly respectful. 'Though I can't say I took any notice at the time.'

'When was this?'

'About five minutes before the doctor arrived, I'd say. Though I can't be sure whether it was before or after I spoke to Mr Langley.'

'And one other thing. Inspector, you said you'd had a bottle of gin sent away to be analysed—'

'And the dregs of a glass, Professor Fen. Yes. But that was just a matter of routine.'

'What it all adds up to,' said Adam slowly, 'is simply this:

that Shorthouse must have committed suicide. This room was watched from ten past eleven onwards – and there was no one except Shorthouse in it when the doctor arrived. But on the medical evidence, it's *impossible* that Shorthouse could have been dead at ten past eleven. His heart certainly wouldn't have gone on beating for *twenty minutes.*'

'Exactly, sir.' The Inspector was displaying something like confidence for the first time that morning. 'Suicide, it seems to me, is the only possible verdict.'

'I wish I could be sure of that.' Fen spoke almost to himself. 'Because I have a vague idea—'

He was interrupted by a knock on the door, which Furbelow opened. A small, ecstatic man was revealed, bearing a briefcase. He rushed in – there is no other word for it – and beamed at everybody with unconcealed pleasure.

'Well, here we are,' he announced, 'laden with all the gory details. Oh, it's been a splendid job, I can tell you. So quick! Such neat incisions! Such meticulous tests!'

'This is Dr Rashmole,' said Mudge helplessly to the company in general.

'I'll be sitting here, I think,' said Dr Rashmole, seizing a chair with sufficient violence to suggest that he wished to frighten it into compliance and good behaviour. 'Now, you'll be anxious to get down to it at once. I have here' – he fumbled in his briefcase – '*as well as* the PM report, the analyst's report on the gin – what a livery drink, to be sure – and something about the clothes, which they gave me at the police station to bring along. How do you do?' he added to Elizabeth.

'Very well, thank you,' said Elizabeth faintly.

'First then' – Dr Rashmole had got out some typewritten sheets – 'the *Cause of Death*: dislocation of the second and third cervical vertebrae. That's the neck,' he explained charitably. 'He got it in the neck. Well, well, no time for jests, no time for jests. The usual *post mortem* appearances – need I define them?'

'No,' Sir Richard put in hastily. 'No.'

'Then quite evidently he took a quantity of some barbiturate drug before he died. Hyperaemia. Oedema of the brain. Degenerative changes in the convoluted tubules of the kidneys, and *cloudy swelling* of the liver. Tchk! Tchk!' Dr Rashmole shook his head in a deprecatory manner. 'We think it's Nembutal, but we can't be certain until further tests have been made. It's a slow business, very slow and wearisome. And then again it might be Soporigene. Does that seem more likely to you?'

'As to that,' Mudge began feebly, but luckily Dr Rashmole gave him no chance to finish.

'Well, we shall soon know,' he said. 'Perhaps there's something about it in the report on the gin. The gen on the gin, as you might say. Well, well, scarcely the occasion for jokes, I suppose. Let's have a look at it.' He produced an envelope, ripped it open with one savage thrust, and pulled out the contents. 'Ah. Nembutal it is. Three hundred grains in the bottle – what a quantity, what a quantity – and thirty in the dregs of the glass.'

'In the bottle?' Fen put in sharply.

'Exactly. Apparently the bottle was only a quarter full . . . Well, I must be off. I'll leave these papers with you.' And Dr Rashmole made for the door.

'Just a minute,' Mudge called hurriedly. 'This Nembutal – it's a soporific, isn't it? It'd knock you out?'

'In that amount,' Dr Rashmole answered. 'I'm surprised it didn't kill him. He had a very lucky escape – very lucky indeed. Well, good morning. Work to be done, work to be done.' He passed out like a wind. The door slammed shatteringly behind him.

'Heavens,' said Elizabeth with feeling. 'Are *all* police doctors like that?'

But Mudge was studying the third report which Dr Rashmole had brought. 'Here's a funny thing,' he said slowly. 'There were traces of rope on Shorthouse's socks – as if his feet had been tied. And on his shirt cuffs.' He hesitated. 'What's to be made of that?'

'Any marks of tying mentioned in the PM report?' Fen asked.

Mudge took up the relevant papers and scrabbled through them. 'Yes . . . "Slight weals on wrists and ankles, possibly caused by tying". It's uncommonly odd.'

'Not as odd as the fact that the gin bottle was doped,' said Fen briskly. 'If it had been only the glass, he might have taken it himself – as a kind of anodyne to what he intended to do. But it's inconceivable that *he* put it in the bottle.'

Adam gazed up at him, mildly. 'Then perhaps you'll kindly tell us,' he said, 'just how one commits an impossible murder.'

Chapter Eight

'Oh, for a beakerful of the cold north,' said Fen, gulping at his Burton. 'Impossible murders, for the present, must wait their turn.'

They were sitting before a blazing and hospitable fire in the small front parlour of the 'Bird and Baby'. Mudge had parted from them, with notable reluctance, at the door, in order to pursue his duties in less congenial circumstances; and Adam, Elizabeth, Sir Richard Freeman, and Fen were now toasting themselves to a comfortable glow. Outside, it was still attempting to snow, but with only partial success.

'Darling, my nose is so cold,' Elizabeth complained to Adam. 'And everything's really very tiresome. What is going to happen about the production?'

'Oh, it'll come off – though later than we thought, I fancy. George Green can sing Sachs. I doubt if it will set the rehearsals back very much – not more than a week, anyway; if that.' Adam drank his beer; it was cold enough to make him shiver a little.

'Professor Fen' – Elizabeth adopted her most politic charm – 'would you be prepared to let me interview you for a newspaper?'

Fen made a feeble attempt to show disinclination. 'Oh, I don't know . . .' he mumbled.

'*Please*, Professor Fen. It's in a series. I'm hoping to do H.M., and Mrs Bradley, and Albert Campion, and all sorts of famous people.'

'Well, this is a surprise,' said Fen, carefully avoiding Adam's eye. A certain uneasiness of manner became apparent. 'But all these people are rather more able than I am . . . Well,' for the moment, he was evidently rather subdued, 'what exactly did you want to know?'

'Just tell me something about your cases.'

In the absence of an appropriate introductory fanfare, Fen coughed impressively. 'The era of my greatest successes,' he began, but was interrupted with singular brutality by Sir Richard Freeman.

'Now,' the latter remarked firmly, 'if we're all warmed up, let's get back to the Shorthouse affair . . . It's very childish to sulk, Gervase . . . So far the central character has been, to me at any rate, somewhat of a cipher. What was Shorthouse like, Langley?'

Adam considered. 'In appearance – stout, not very tall; rather small eyes; self-confident; a bit of a hypochondriac, particularly about his voice; age between forty and fifty, I should say.' He paused and drank some beer. 'As regards character – well, I must admit I didn't like him. I scarcely think anyone did. He was a trouble-maker – and his love-life wasn't exactly idyllic, I may add.'

'There goes C. S. Lewis,' said Fen suddenly. 'It must be Tuesday.'

'It is Tuesday.' Sir Richard struck a match and puffed doggedly at his pipe.

'You seem to smoke the most incombustible tobacco,'

Fen commented. 'The era of my greatest successes—'

'In what way a trouble-maker?' Sir Richard pushed at the tobacco in the bowl of his pipe and burned his fingers. 'Can you give us an example?'

Adam narrated in some detail the events of yesterday's rehearsal.

'We were all a trifle nervous,' he concluded, 'about what was going to happen this morning. You see, Edwin had said he was going to phone Levi and try to get Peacock replaced. Consequently . . .'

He stopped hastily.

'Ah.' Fen slowly nodded his head, mandarin-like. 'That's the word. "Consequently". It appears—'

'It appears,' said Sir Richard, interrupting him, 'that Peacock would have a motive for murdering Shorthouse. *Did* Shorthouse telephone Levi, by the way?'

'I don't know,' said Adam, 'but I very much doubt it. If he had, I should have weighed in on Peacock's side, and we should have had a general explosion of artistic tempera-ment.'

'You chivalrous old thing,' said Elizabeth affectionately.

Fen, who had been singing to himself a hideous parody of Pogner's Address, said:

'And this young man you noticed at the rehearsal yesterday – you think he was the one who visited Shorthouse's dressing-room last night?'

'I presume so.'

'You presume so,' Fen looked despondent. 'Well, we shall soon find out, I've no doubt.'

'He may have a motive, too.' Sir Richard gazed into the bowl of his pipe as though he expected to see a serpent there. He then shook it, irritably. 'That is' – he gestured vaguely

– 'this girl. What you said, Langley, suggests that she's a link between Boris Who-ever-he-is and Shorthouse.'

'*Cherchez la femme,*' said Fen tediously.

'It's possible,' Adam answered. 'But personally I know nothing about it. Joan Davis would be the person to ask.'

'That's the girl who's singing Eva, isn't it?'

Adam gurgled an affirmative through his beer. '*Darling,*' said Elizabeth reproachfully.

'We've got two possible suspects so far, then,' said Fen. 'Peacock and Boris Godunov, or whatever his name is. We've also got a situation in which a man is murdered with no one in the room . . . Can you hang a man at a distance?'

'Through the skylight, perhaps,' Adam suggested. 'It opens, doesn't it?'

'You'd have to transfer him to the hook afterwards,' said Elizabeth practically. 'Which is scarcely possible – from outside.'

Adam sighed and glanced at the door of the bar. It opened to admit a large, articulated human skeleton. After it came Mudge, grasping it about the waist. For the moment they were unnerved. A woman in another corner of the bar gave a little shriek.

'And whose cupboard,' said Fen, 'did you find that in?' He laughed heartily. When he had stopped:

'Really, Mudge,' said Sir Richard sternly, 'whatever your enthusiasm for the case, this is going a little far. You haven't walked through the streets of Oxford with that thing, have you?'

Mudge was abashed. 'I came in the car, sir,' he said in subdued tones; then, brightening: 'But look – look at its neck.'

They looked at its neck. Everyone in the bar looked at its

neck. There was no doubt that something had given it a very nasty wrench indeed.

'It would seem' – Mudge was triumphant – 'it would seem as though there had been a rehearsal beforehand.'

With a certain amount of tumult the skeleton was pushed out of the way under one of the wooden benches. 'And if anyone says "Alas, poor Yorick",' Fen announced, 'there will be a second murder.' Mudge was given beer. His manner was penitential, and he eyed the Chief Constable with such manifest unease that Fen was driven to pat him encouragingly on the back.

Some discussion followed, which was scarcely enlightening. The skeleton had been found in the property-room of the opera-house, where normally it belonged; but no one, and least of all Furbelow, had been able to account for the accident to its neck. 'There was one point in the PM report,' said Mudge, 'and that was that the dislocation seems to have been the result of considerable violence; almost as though someone had jumped up and clung to him while he was hanging, so as to weigh him down.'

There was a sudden silence: then, 'How horrible,' Elizabeth remarked in a small voice.

'Surely there's no opera a skeleton comes into,' said Fen.

'Oh, yes.' Adam nodded. 'It comes in Charles Shorthouse's opera on Kaiser's *Morn to Midnight*. By the way, I suppose Charles will inherit Edwin's money.'

'Isn't he well off?'

'He was, but I think he spent most of his capital financing his own operas. You know, of course, that no one can possibly make a *living* by writing operas – at any rate in England,' Adam mused. 'Edwin must have accumulated a few thousand;

and as he isn't married, I imagine they'll go to Charles, and pay for the staging of the *Oresteia*.'

'The *Oresteia*?'

'It's a big tetralogy he's just finishing: Cadogan's done the libretto. Apparently it pretty well needs a new theatre built to do it in – a second Bayreuth, as it were.'

'Then Charles Shorthouse is a suspect,' said Fen with a certain satisfaction. 'There goes C. S. Lewis again.'

'Except that he lives at Amersham,' Sir Richard interposed.

'There is transport. Obviously we shall have to find out what he was doing last night. He may have an alibi.'

By now the little bar was beginning to empty again, as people drifted out for lunch. The opening of the door admitted blasts of cold wind, and they could just glimpse the grey stone front of St John's standing against a sky of more luminous grey, and tall, bare trees, spattered with little wisps of white, and one of the robot-like lampposts which are lined along the centre of St Giles'. It was growing so dark as to seem like evening. In the halls of Colleges, tasteless soups or sinister, bloated sausages, reminiscent of financiers in a socialist cartoon, were being set on tables. Fen's thoughts were turning to food.

'My thoughts,' he told them, 'are turning to food.'

'And my feet,' said Elizabeth firmly, 'are turning to ice . . . Adam darling, I supose you realize you're keeping *all* the fire off me?'

Two newcomers entered the bar. Adam, caught midway in a complex movement which drew wails of annoyance from Fen, greeted them in a harassed and absent manner. They drew near, diffidently.

'Come and share the fire,' said Sir Richard agreeably.

The young man smiled in tacit apology for disturbing them. He was handsome in a dark, foreign fashion, and wiry, with alert, imaginative eyes, but his face was disfigured by some sort of skin disease, and he looked far from well. With him was Judith Haynes. Though she was very young, her manner was aloof and mistrustful, with a veneer of sophistication which gave evidence of careful cultivation. Beneath a heavy brown coat she wore slacks and a jersey which emphasized the slenderness, almost the fragility, of her figure. A few flecks of half-melted snow glittered in her fair hair. She stood a little behind the young man, watching him with a trace of anxiety in her eyes. It was not difficult to see that she was very much in love with him.

'Let me introduce you,' said Adam, suddenly mindful of his responsibilities. 'Mr –?'

'Stapleton,' said the young man. 'Boris Stapleton. And this is Judith Haynes.'

'My wife,' Adam responded. 'Professor Fen, Sir Richard Freeman, Inspector Mudge.' It was as though he were reeling off a list of malefactors.

A conventional murmur of gratification went up. Hierophantically, Fen rearranged the circle round the fire and ordered a new round of drinks. A momentary blankness fell upon all their minds. It was clear, too, that the potential relevance of Stapleton to the matter in hand had not revealed itself to Mudge. He was finishing his beer in surreptitious haste, plainly considering that the time for his departure had arrived. Adam observed this.

'Miss Haynes and Mr Stapleton' – his tones were significantly informative – 'are both in *Die Meistersinger*.'

Mudge became instantly less fretful. He opened his mouth to speak, but Stapleton unwittingly forestalled him.

'What's going to happen, sir?' he asked of Adam. 'Will the first night be postponed?'

'I imagine so.' Adam nodded. 'But I haven't seen Peacock this morning. I heard from Joan, though, that Levi has been telephoned, and is in a condition approaching apoplexy.'

'It's extraordinary.' Stapleton's utterance seemed less conventional than genuinely perplexed. 'The more so as I myself saw Mr Shorthouse quite late last night.'

The name of Shorthouse roused Mudge into activity. He joined the conversation, cautiously, like a toreador confronted by a particularly incalculable bull.

'I gather, Mr Stapleton,' he said, 'that you were the last person to see Mr Shorthouse alive?'

Stapleton hesitated, fractionally. 'Was I? I've heard no details, I'm afraid. Certainly I was with him last evening.'

'Really, now? May I ask *why* you visited him, sir?'

'It was about my opera. He'd agreed to look at the score. I went to ask him what he thought of it.'

'Surely rather a late hour, sir, for a discussion of that kind?'

'It was his suggestion,' Stapleton said helplessly. 'I was scarcely in a position to object.'

'Ah,' said Mudge. 'But you agree it was a queer time for him to choose?'

'Oh, yes, I agree.' Stapleton looked uncomfortable. 'But still – there it is.'

Mudge grunted uncivilly, and asked:

'Have you any idea, sir, what Mr Shorthouse himself was doing in the theatre at that hour?'

'Well, when I arrived,' said Stapleton frankly, 'he wasn't doing anything except drinking gin.'

'I mean, didn't it strike you as odd that he should ask you to discuss the matter *there*, rather than at – well, wherever he lived?'

'Yes, it did.' Stapleton's ready acquiescence in all these

peculiarities was mildly disconcerting. 'But I simply assumed he had some special reason for being at the theatre.'

'I see.' Mudge comtemplated resignedly this barren subject, and turned to other matters. 'Now, I understand from Furbelow that you were only with Mr Shorthouse a few minutes.'

'Yes.' Stapleton's answers were of the discouraging sort which throw all the burden on the interlocutor, but his manner was perfectly inoffensive.

'Then – then' – Mudge looked round him rather wildly, in an effort to remember what he had been going to say – 'there was no one else in Mr Shorthouse's dressing-room during the time you were there?'

'No one.'

'And you talked about—'

'About my opera. He was vague and condescending – praising with faint damns, as it were. As a matter of fact, I'm certain he hadn't even glanced at it. He didn't return me the score, by the way – I suppose it's still at his lodgings.'

'After you left him you went home?'

'Yes.'

'Where are you staying, Mr Stapleton?'

'In Clarendon Street. Quite near the theatre. Judith's in the same house.'

'Ah, yes. Miss Haynes, did you see or hear Mr Stapleton come in?'

'No.' Judith flushed, as though she had been accused of some impropriety. 'I must have been in bed by that time.'

'Did Shorthouse strike you as being in a suicidal frame of mind, Stapleton?' Fen spoke a little absently; he was engaged in lighting a new cigarette from the end of the first.

'I don't think so.' Stapleton grimaced expressively. 'From

what *I* knew of him, he wasn't the man to commit suicide, either.' He hesitated, and then went on: 'The only odd thing I noticed about him was that he seemed scarcely able to keep awake. I suppose he must have drunk too much.'

Mudge raised his eyebrows, but forbore to comment, and in fact, Adam reflected, there was little to say; Stapleton might be telling the truth, or again, he might be telling a deliberate lie, in order to conceal the fact that he himself had doped the gin while he was in with Shorthouse. There seemed no way of deciding. One thing, however, was evident enough: that in order to hang an able-bodied man one must render him powerless first, and that this could be effected either by tying him up or by dosing him with Nembutal. But why – on the evidence – both? Certainly one or other of them seemed to be superfluous.

'It *must* have been suicide, you know,' Elizabeth put in. 'Murder – well, I mean, it's just impossible. Or is it?' She frowned. 'Really,' she said, 'it's as though the laws of gravity were suspended . . .'

Apparently, however, Mudge had no comment to make on this. He returned to the attack.

'And about your movements earlier in the evening?' he said to Stapleton.

Stapleton raised his glass and drank before replying; it was not inconceivable that he wanted time to consider. 'About nine o'clock,' he said, 'I left my digs in Clarendon Street, where I'd been reading since dinner-time, and went to the "Gloucester" for a drink; talked to one or two of the Playhouse people until closing-time; then went for a walk and eventually came back to the theatre at eleven to see Shorthouse.'

'A walk,' Mudge repeated resignedly. 'Alone, I suppose?'

'Alone. It wasn't a bad evening. There was even a scrap of moon.'

'Very well, sir. And was there anyone at your lodgings who could swear to the time you eventually got in?'

'I doubt it. I'd arranged with my landlady that as I was likely to be late I should lock the door after me when I came in, so presumably she'd already gone to bed. But someone may have heard me. As a matter of fact, after I left Shorthouse I went for another walk.'

'*Another* walk?' Mudge stared, seemingly distressed at such lack of variety.

'Another walk,' Stapleton assured him solemnly. 'Not a long one, on this occasion. I must have got home about twenty to midnight.'

Mudge inhaled deeply; he was on the point of speech when Fen forestalled him.

'You didn't talk to Shorthouse at all,' Fen asked amiably, 'about Miss Haynes?'

Chapter Nine

The girl turned quickly to look at him, the electric light flashing momentarily on her fair hair.

'Why should they have talked about me?' she said, and was angry at the slight trembling of her voice.

Fen regarded her thoughtfully. 'Perhaps it's rather a delicate matter,' he said. 'But in the circumstances, people are bound to hear about it sooner or later . . . I understood that Shorthouse was – well, let us say, attracted to you.'

Judith was rather pale. 'I suppose,' she stammered, 'one might – No, I—'

She stopped, embarrassed and confused. And Mudge closed the uneasy gap with unexpected smoothness and finesse.

'Naturally,' he cooed, with such a wealth of oily tact that Sir Richard stopped fidgeting with his pipe and stared – 'naturally it's a thing we should be bound to look into in the course of an investigation like this. And since secondhand accounts are always distasteful' – he waved a hand in rather histrionic deprecation – 'it's better that we should hear what there is to hear from you.'

Stapleton said: 'Darling, I don't think you're obliged—' but before he could finish the girl interrupted him.

'The Inspector's quite right,' she said in a low voice. 'It's bound to come out. And anyway, there's nothing to conceal . . .'

'You see, Boris and I are lovers' – she tried to speak as if this were the most natural thing in the world, and failed – 'and Mr Shorthouse had been making – well, I believe one calls them "advances". That's all. Naturally I didn't encourage him.'

'"Advances"?' Mudge queried with glassy incomprehension.

Judith flushed, and answered more loudly than was necessary. 'I don't mean he wanted to marry me. Quite the reverse. He wanted me to be his mistress.'

Mudge made clicking sounds of an objurgatory kind, and shook his head. He seemed appropriately impressed. 'But you, Mr Stapleton,' he persisted. 'You of course resented this?'

'Not at all,' the girl broke in before Stapleton could reply. 'Our reactions aren't quite so primitive, Inspector. We merely laughed at the whole business.'

But Stapleton was firm. 'It isn't as simple as that, darling.'

He turned to the Inspector. 'I did resent it – yes. But since Shorthouse was – well, what he was, I didn't feel so very distressed. One doesn't bother much about burglars so long as they've no chance of getting into one's own house.'

Mudge gravely indicated his appreciation of this rather anti-social sentiment.

'And now, Miss,' he said to Judith, 'I wonder if you'd mind telling me about *your* movements last night?'

'I was in all evening, alone, and I went to bed at half past ten.'

'That seems straightforward enough. And you say you didn't at all resent Mr Shorthouse's – ah – suggestions?'

Judith shrugged. 'That sort of thing happens, you know.'

'Just so.' Mudge exuded worldly sympathy. 'Well, I think I needn't trouble you any further for the present. Unless there's anything Professor Fen would like to ask?'

Professor Fen, however, was at least partially comatose. He roused himself with difficulty.

'No, nothing,' he said after a certain amount of reflection. '*Schön Dank, mein Jung*', he sang as an afterthought.

'And we must go,' Stapleton finished his beer and threw the end of his cigarette into the fire. 'Or we shall never get any lunch.'

Judith stood up, wrapping her coat round her, and Stapleton took her arm, giving it a friendly little squeeze.

'Oh, Mr Langley,' – she spoke hesitantly, as they turned towards the door – 'did Miss Davis say anything to you about Boris's opera?'

'She did indeed.' Adam smiled at her. 'I should very much like to look at it.'

'You'll be disappointed, I'm afraid,' said Stapleton with youthful seriousness. 'But it's most kind of you, nonetheless.'

'When can I have it?'

'I suppose it's still among Shorthouse's possessions.' Stapleton looked dubiously at Mudge. 'Perhaps the Inspector—'

'I'll hand it over,' Mudge assured him, 'after I've been through his stuff. Unless, of course' – he became momentarily jocose – 'I find it has some special bearing on the crime.'

'But don't expect me to get it put on, even if I like it,' Adam said. 'You know as well as I do how little chance there is of that . . . By the way, it is a vocal score, I hope. Liszt is supposed to have played the whole of *Tristan* at sight from the full orchestral score, but I'm not up to *that* standard.'

'I fancy it's a legend.' Stapleton was interested. 'I don't believe even Liszt could have done it . . . No, it is a vocal score. Oh, and I must return that removing-cream you lent me.'

'Keep it,' said Adam. Judith and Stapleton made their farewells and departed into the outer cold.

'Removing-cream?' Elizabeth inquired. 'Not that expensive jar I bought for you during *Don Pasquale*?'

Adam reassured her. 'I gave him the one which Edwin tried to pinch. I haven't been using it myself.'

'They're a nice couple,' said Fen thoughtfully. 'And very much in love, it would seem. But the girl's suffering from nerves, and Stapleton looks as if he ought to see a doctor . . . I wonder if she disliked Shorthouse's deplorable proposals as little as she pretended.'

'You mean,' Mudge queried, 'that she might have had a motive for killing him?'

'There's a kind of physical revulsion' – Fen was speaking almost to himself – 'which could possibly drive a girl like that to murder. I believe any suggestion of promiscuous sensuality would repel her violently. Anyway, one can't rule it out altogether. And one can't rule out the possibility that Stapleton resented Shorthouse's behaviour to the point of homicide. It really seems to depend on just how far Shorthouse went.' He paused. 'That gives us four motives: Peacock (his career, *via* the production), Charles Shorthouse (money), Stapleton (vengeance), and Judith Haynes (offended virtue). And what are the problems? First, why Shorthouse was tied, as well as doped with Nembutal? Second, who phoned Shand, and why? Third, what was Shorthouse doing in the theatre at that hour?'

'You forget the real problem,' said Adam. 'That is, how anyone could manage to kill Shorthouse *at all*.'

'I have the beginnings of an idea about that,' Fen replied, 'though I must admit I don't see – well, never mind. I must visit Charles Shorthouse. Adam, do you know him?'

'A little.'

'Good. Come with me. We'll have lunch, and then drive to Amersham.'

Chapter Ten

So Sir Richard returned to his house on Boar's Hill, and Mudge went esoterically about his business. Fen, Adam, and Elizabeth lunched in Fen's room at St Christopher's. It was a large room in the second quadrangle, reached by a short flight of carpeted stairs which led up from an alley-way giving access to the gardens. It was, as the saying goes, 'lined with books'; Chinese miniatures were on the walls; and various dilapidated plaques and busts of the greater masters of English Literature decorated the mantelpiece. They ate off a noble Sheraton table, and were served by Fen's scout.

They talked about opera, and in particular about Wagner; speculations about the death of Shorthouse had inevitably reached a stasis for want of further information. Over coffee, they considered plans for the afternoon.

'I certainly shan't come to Amersham,' said Elizabeth. 'It's far too cold. How soon will you be going?'

'Almost at once, I should think.' Fen looked at his watch. 'Two o'clock. It'll take us at least an hour to get there, even in Lily Christine.'

'I suppose you're a safe driver,' Adam remarked gloomily. He was rather nervous of cars. 'What will you do with yourself, darling?'

'Go to a film, I should think,' Elizabeth answered. 'Or fall asleep beside the fire. You'll be back when?'

'Between tea and dinner, with any luck,' said Fen. 'We'll see you then.'

It was not until they were properly under way that Adam recognized the force of that 'with any luck'. They would require a great deal of luck, he thought, sitting petrified in the front seat, if they were to get back at all. To realize that anyone is not a very good driver takes a little time; the mind is not eager, in the face of a long journey to accept this particular verity; and it was not until Fen emerged into the High Street, with the velocity of a benighted traveller pursued by spectres, that Adam became really alarmed.

'Be careful!' he shouted. 'Be careful, or something will get us!'

'It's perfectly all right,' said Fen, hauling on the wheel in a split-second manoeuvre between two buses which made Adam go cold all over. 'I never take any risks.' He rushed between a cart and a lorry with about half an inch to spare on either side. 'It simply doesn't seem to me to be worth it.'

Adam said nothing – there was, indeed, nothing to say – but sat as rigid as if he had been confronted by the Gorgon's head. The car rushed on towards Headington. It was a small, red, battered and extremely noisy sports car; a chilled-looking female nude in chromium projected from its radiator cap; across its bonnet were scrawled in large white letters the words LILY CHRISTINE III.

'I bought her,' said Fen, removing both hands from the wheel in order to search for a cigarette, 'from an undergraduate who was sent down. But of course she was laid up during the war, and I don't think it's improved her.' He shook his head, sombrely. 'Things keep falling out of the engine,' he explained.

The three-quarters of an hour which elapsed before they arrived at High Wycombe, Adam occupied with repenting, in some detail, the moral imperfections of his past life. By the time they had left the main road, and were climbing the hill which leads to Amersham, he was sufficiently resigned to be capable of conversation again.

'Tell me,' said Fen, 'is Charles Shorthouse married?'

'No,' Adam replied. 'He lives in what is reputed to be sin' – at this point Fen's negotiation of a particularly acute bend aroused in him afresh the fear of eternal torment – 'I mean, *reputedly* he lives in *sin* with a woman called Beatrix Thorn. She is not attractive,' Adam added unchivalrously. 'She is not attractive at all. But composers have a way of getting hold of the most appalling women. I can never quite see why it is. Look at the Princess Wittgenstein. Look at Mlle Recio. Look at Cosima. Look at—'

'All right,' said Fen. 'I accept the general proposition.' He changed gear with a sound like a dragon in torment. 'Then those two make up the ménage?'

'There's also an amanuensis. I forget his name. He does the piano scores of the operas. And then there are hangers-on of one sort and another.' Adam frowned, in the effort of giving definition to this woolly asseveration. 'Kept critics; admirers; parasites.'

'What would you say was Shorthouse's standing as a composer?'

'Pretty high,' Adam admitted reluctantly. 'On a par with Walton and Vaughan Williams, anyway. Whether he deserves it is another matter; I'm inclined to think not. He's a kind of Salieri to their Mozart – or a Meyerbeer to their Wagner.'

'And he disliked Edwin?'

'Very much. As far as I know, there wasn't any special reason for it, though; a purely temperamental antipathy. They saw very little of one another, in any case.'

The road widened. A sand-pit flashed by on their right hand, dark ochre under the grey sky. They entered a beech-wood, dank and cavernous, the ground carpeted with rotting leaves. Through tangles of briar and dead bracken there were glimpses of deep dells. By a deserted, rickety cottage, its windows blank and its hedges untrimmed, they turned off to the left.

'Nearly there,' Fen murmured.

They came out of the wood, and a few hundred yards farther on arrived at a tall gate with an old lodge beside it.

'This is it,' said Adam. 'It's a sharp turn,' he announced with considerably more urgency, 'and the ground's very wet . . .'

A grinding shock accompanied their entry into the drive. In Adam's imagination the flames of the pit crackled with horrifying imminence. But Fen did not stop; the flames receded.

'It's only a wing,' said Fen without much perturbation. 'Goodness, what a clatter it's making. I suppose it must have worked loose.'

Creating a din like a gang of riveters on Clydeside, they sped up the short gravel drive. In another moment the house came in view.

It was an unspectacular building, large, modern, two-storied, constructed of red brick. The drive curved to the right and ended in a sundial surrounded by spiky-looking lavender bushes. Fen stopped just short of this, and switched off the ignition. After a moment the car backfired, and then, as if unsatisfied with the first attempt, backfired again, much more loudly.

'It's funny she still does that,' said Fen, interested. 'I've never been able to make out the reason for it. Well, let's have a look at the damage.'

But they were given no opportunity to do this. A small, savage-looking woman with a long nose and a harsh voice rushed suddenly out of the front door and up to them.

'The noise,' she hissed vehemently. '*The noise*. Have you no consideration for the Master?' She paused, her beady eyes almost popping out of her head with annoyance. '*Mr Langley*: you at least should know. *All cars must be left outside the gates*. Who *knows* what damage your uproar may have done to the Master's work?'

'Uproar?' Fen repeated, greatly offended. 'Lily Christine is a very quiet-running car. I admit,' he added handsomely, 'that the wing was making rather a noise, but then you'd make a noise if you'd just been torn off by a gatepost.'

'The precise *cause* of the disturbance,' snapped the small woman, 'is scarcely relevant. It's the *result* that matters. The Master's brain is a highly delicate instrument; the least shock may unhinge it – no, I don't mean that, of course . . .'

'Well, whatever you mean,' said Fen, tiring abruptly of this subject, 'we want to see Mr Shorthouse.'

'*Im*possible,' said the small woman with furious emphasis. 'Completely *im*possible. The Master is working and must not be disturbed.'

'Please, Miss Thorn.' Adam was cajoling. 'It's really a matter of some urgency.'

'*Im*possible. The Master can only be seen by appointment.'

'We've travelled a considerable distance, Miss Thorn.'

'Mr Langley, if you had travelled from Mars the situation would be no different.'

'Look here,' said Fen, who was liable to resort to unlikely impostures when in any difficulty, 'I represent the Metropolitan Opera House, New York. I wish to negotiate with Mr Shorthouse for the *Oresteia*.'

'Ha!' exclaimed Miss Thorn sharply; it was as though she had suddenly caught sight of a vampire. 'Mr Langley, is this true?'

Under the compulsion of Fen's malignant blue eye, Adam admitted that this was true.

'Then,' said Miss Thorn, mollified, but still a little suspicious, 'you must come in. Please keep to carpets, and avoid tramping your feet on the bare boards. *The least noise* . . . And I should be obliged if you would pitch your voices to the faintest whisper.'

'Oh,' said Fen, momentarily awed by these directions. 'Oh.' They went inside.

Though preternaturally quiet, the house gave marked evidence of the vehement demeanour of its *châtelaine*. Everything conveyed the impression of furious activity transfixed in mid-career. A bronze Mercury strained savagely upwards from his ballasting pedestal; on a large canvas, the Eumenides were represented fairly whisking along against a background of embattled cohorts; Beethoven glowered from a wall-bracket; a stuffed panther was in the act of hurling itself, open-mouthed, on some incautious denizen of the jungle; Laocoön, marble-limbed, struggled eternally in his coils; St George, with lance uplifted and muscles tense, would never, it was obvious, succeed in dispatching his dragon; and in one corner of the hall a furious-looking cat was trying to get at a parrot. It was far from restful; indeed, it was almost apoplectic. Though he had seen it all before, and hence might consider himself to some extent acclimatized, Adam was unable to repress a shudder.

Miss Thorn, striding unperturbed through this ghostly tumult, conducted them into a small back room. Here she turned to face Fen.

'Well?' she inquired in a hoarse whisper.

'Well?' Fen countered blankly. 'Where is Mr Shorthouse?' He gazed suspiciously at a large urn whose sides were stencilled with an energetic Rape of the Sabine Women, as though expecting that the composer might be concealed within it.

'All the Master's business affairs,' hissed Miss Thorn, 'pass through my hands. You may speak freely to me.'

'Oh, I may, may I?' said Fen, who was not possessed of much patience at the best of times. 'But I'm sorry to say I have no authority to deal with anyone but Mr Shorthouse himself.'

'*Im*possible.'

'Then I shall go back to America,' Fen announced with conviction.

'If you could wait an hour or so . . .'

'No,' said Fen, on whose normal tones an American accent had rather implausibly grafted itself during the foregoing interchange. '*Im*possible,' he added involuntarily. 'I have to see Richard Strauss – *almost at once*.' He frowned with such severity that Miss Thorn, who, Adam suspected, was essentially a credulous soul, was visibly shaken.

'Well,' she whispered, 'I suppose we *might* disturb the Master . . .'

'Let us by all means disturb the Master. I don't doubt he'll be most annoyed if you keep me from him.'

This was a hit, a palpable hit; it was evident that the last thing Miss Thorn wanted was the Master's disfavour. She drew a deep breath, like one about to plunge into cold water.

'Wait,' she said, 'I shall be back shortly.'

They waited; she was back shortly. 'Will you come this way,' she said; it was less a question than an awestruck comment on their transcendent good fortune. 'The Master will see you.'

They returned through the hall. How nice it would be, thought Adam, if by this time Consummation had supervened – Mercury flown, the Eumenides vanished, the panther quiescent and satiated, Laocoön dead, the dragon dispatched. But no; all were fixed and immutable in their rage, as before; and Adam shuddered again as Miss Thorn led them up the staircase. Her manner suggested that the Veil of the Temple was about to be put aside; she walked on tip-toe, with elaborate precautions against noise.

It was not long before they reached the door of the Holy of Holies. Miss Thorn opened it reverently and peered inside. A peevish voice said:

'Well, come along, come along.'

Another moment, and they were in the Presence. The Presence, it should be said, displayed no special desire for Miss Thorn's continued company.

'All right, Beatrix,' it said testily. 'I can manage.'

'You're quite sure?'

'Of course I'm sure. Leave me alone with these gentlemen.'

'Very well, Master. Don't tire yourself.'

'I am perfectly fit.'

'I wasn't suggesting, Master, that you weren't perfectly fit. But you mustn't exhaust yourself unnecessarily.'

'Will you go away, Beatrix.'

'Very well, Master. If you need me, you have only to call.'

'It's very unlikely that I shall need you.'

'But you might.'

'In that case I'll call. Now please leave us.'

Sighing, Miss Thorn departed. The Master advanced to greet them. He was a small, plump, middle-aged man with a large head and horn-rimmed spectacles, and he looked harassed.

'Nice to meet you,' he said; his voice held the faintest suggestion of Cockney. 'I expect you'd like to hear some of my *Oresteia*. Can either of you sing?'

'Surely you remember me, Shorthouse?' said Adam, annoyed.

'Oh, *Langley*. Of course. How stupid of me. Are you going over to the Metropolitan? We're losing all our native singers nowadays . . . Well, I'll play you the second act of the *Agamemnon*, if you like. That'll give you an idea of the work as a whole.'

'This is Professor Fen, from Oxford.'

'Glad to meet you. Very progressive of the Metropolitan to employ an educated man as their agent.'

'No, no . . . Professor Fen has nothing to do with the Metropolitan.'

'Beatrix distinctly said . . .'

'It was a ruse,' Adam explained. 'She wouldn't let us in at first.'

'I'm not surprised, either,' said the Master; and then, evidently feeling that this might sound ungracious, added: 'What I mean is, she lets very few people in at the best of times.' He had crossed to the window and was contemplating Lily Christine. 'What a nice little car. I wish,' he said wistfully, 'that I could have a nice little car like that.'

'Surely you could if you wanted one.'

'No. Beatrix wouldn't let me. She's very anxious to protect me from noise. People creep about this house, you know, as though one were lying dead. It becomes unnerving after a time . . . Well, do sit down, if you can find anywhere.'

For the moment this was a problem, since the room was less untidy than chaotic. It was dominated by a Steinway grand piano, and every available surface was littered with music manuscript paper. Over by the window was a tall wooden desk at which the Master stood while scoring; quantities of bedraggled hothouse flowers drooped from vases; and a photograph of Beatrix Thorn and the Master gazing at one another, rather self-consciously, hung crookedly on the wall. Fen and Adam cleared a couple of chairs and sat on them; the Master paced up and down.

'I've really lost all control,' he was saying. 'Beatrix doesn't want me to be worried with domestic details, so I can never find out what's going on. For example' – he shook his head, mystified – 'there seems to be a huge number of maidservants, who whenever you meet them are always either tear-stained or actually weeping. I used to think Beatrix was responsible for this, but I've discovered recently that it's Gabriel, my amanuensis, who has a penchant for the opposite sex. I can't think,' he added with great frankness, 'what he does to them . . . By the way, did you come to see me about anything in particular?'

'Yes,' said Adam. 'About your brother.'

'Oh, Edwin.' The Master was not enthusiastic. 'And how is the dear fellow?'

'You must know he's dead.'

'So he is,' said the Master, brightening. 'I had a telegram about it this morning. Well, well. When is the funeral? I don't expect I shall get to it, though.'

'It's thought that he was murdered.'

The Master frowned. 'Murdered? What an extraordinary coincidence.'

'Whatever do you mean, coincidence?'

'I'll tell you something' – the Master leaned forward confidingly – 'provided you don't let it go any further.'

'Well?' Fen asked. He appeared stupefied by so much cold-bloodedness.

'I had seriously considered killing Edwin myself.'

Adam gazed at him, aghast. 'You can't mean that?'

'Of course,' the Master admitted, 'I had to consider the pros and cons.' Here Fen muttered something unintelligible, and hastily lit a cigarette. 'The question really was whether Edwin's *voice* or Edwin's *money* was going to be more useful to me in producing the *Oresteia*. I won't say it wasn't a difficult decision to have to make. Edwin was a very fine singer – very fine. It seemed, in a way, a great pity to have to sacrifice him. But' – the Master waved his hand in a simple gesture of resignation – 'first things must come first. And the dilemma, after all, was entirely of his own making. If he had voluntarily offered to finance the *Oresteia*, of course it would not have arisen.'

'You felt' – Adam spoke very cautiously – 'no kind of scruples?'

'Well, of course,' said the Master handsomely, 'one's always a little upset when an emergency of that kind arises. And I confess that when it came to the point I hadn't the heart to go on with it. I postponed the matter – out of sheer moral cowardice, I'm sorry to say. I can hardly forgive myself now. Still, all has turned out for the best. There's a Providence watching over us, as I've always maintained.' And he gazed up at the ceiling, as though expecting actually to see this benignant spirit at its tutelary task.

'And what exactly,' Fen inquired in a strained, unnatural voice, 'was your plan?'

'I went into the matter with some care,' said the Master. He nodded at a row of detective novels and criminological works reposing on a shelf. 'One oughtn't to go about these things in an amateurish way – otherwise the police are liable to find out what has happened. It seems, for example, that one's fingers leave a *distinctive mark* on certain textures and surfaces – a most interesting point . . . However, I won't weary you with an account of my preliminary studies. The first action I took was to write a note to Edwin asking him to meet me at the theatre last night. I thought,' the Master explained, 'that that would constitute a rather less public *mise en scène* than his hotel.'

'But surely he must have considered such an arrangement rather odd?'

'Oh, dear.' The Master was taken aback. 'I hadn't thought of that. Perhaps he did. It's conceivable, of course, that he never turned up there at all. Certainly he sent no reply to my note.'

'You didn't see him, then?'

'No. As I told you, my resolution gave out. Beatrix and I left here at nine o'clock in the Vauxhall – it's a big, purring thing,' the Master informed them aggrievedly, 'not at all like that nice little car you've got. And we arrived in Oxford at half past ten, I suppose. It was then that my resolution failed me. We went to the "Mace and Sceptre" with a friend of mine, and drank coffee. Then at about midnight we left and drove back here again.'

'Were you and Miss Thorn together all the time?'

'I suppose so,' said the Master vaguely, 'I'm not sure that I can remember, really . . . I've an idea that Beatrix and I

lost one another at one stage in the evening; and to be candid'
– he lowered his voice to an apprehensive whisper and glanced
furtively at the door – 'I wasn't altogether sorry. Still, that's
another story.'

Fen sighed, and fidgeted with his feet. 'What is your friend's
name?'

'Wilkes,' said the Master. 'A very charming fellow. You
should look him up if you're ever in Oxford.'

'*Wilkes*,' said Fen with deep disgust. He expelled breath
in a serpentine hiss. 'I know him.'

'Splendid, splendid.'

'And how' – Fen hesitated, in great embarrassment – 'how
did you actually intend to – ah – to deal with your brother?'

'A knife,' said the Master dramatically. 'I had provided
myself with a knife. And I was proposing to jiggle it about
in the wound,' he added, 'so that no one could tell what size
blade had been used.'

Fen rose hastily. 'Well, we must be off,' he said.

The Master was mildly perplexed. 'You wouldn't like to
hear some of the *Oresteia*?'

'I'm afraid we haven't the time.'

'Well then, you must let me know when the Metropolitan
proposes to put it on.'

'No, no, Shorthouse,' said Adam. 'Professor Fen has
nothing to do with the Metropolitan.'

The Master shook his head sadly. 'Stupid of me,' he said.
'There are times when I almost wonder if I'm not getting a
little absent-minded.'

He opened the door for them. In the corridor outside a
maid flitted by, silently weeping.

'There,' said the Master. 'You see? I suppose I ought to
talk to Gabriel about it. The trouble is, though, that as one

gets older one forgets about these things, except in broad outline . . . Well, good afternoon to you. You'll let me have the American agreement sometime, won't you? You needn't be afraid my terms will be at all harsh . . .?'

And the Master retired triumphantly into his room.

Chapter Eleven

Elizabeth had seen Fen and Adam off from the main gate of St Christopher's; and as the tumult of Lily Christine III died away in Broad Street, she began almost to wish that she had gone with them. Oxford in vacation-time has a certain hollow-ness – imparts a sense almost of anticlimax. The occasional don or scout or undergraduate to be seen wandering about the quadrangles serves only to emphasize the echoing vacancy about him. Minatory pronouncements, in thick black type, warn the public that it is no longer permissible to enter the college gardens; porters, slumbering in over-heated lodges, are so rarely disturbed that any intrusion on their quiet rouses them to positive offensiveness; sung services, in the various chapels, degenerate with startling abruptness from a plethora to a definite scarcity, and the clergy are to be found droning away to exiguous congregations of surreptitiously yawning *dévots*; while on normally crowded noticeboards a few belated placards, their edges curling with neglect, flap dismally in the breeze, and one may see an occasional roped trunk, overlooked by the railway, accumulating dust amid a clutter of red-painted fire-buckets and sandbags.

Cumulatively, these things are depressing, and Elizabeth was a little downcast as she stood gazing up St Giles' after her departing husband. She might, she thought, go back to the 'Mace and Sceptre', there to spend the afternoon reading; she might rummage for books in Blackwell's; she might go to the cinema . . . But in her present restless mood none of these things held much immediate attraction. She decided at last to re-visit Somerville, her old college, and accordingly set off along the Woodstock Road.

The expedition, however, proved barren. A porteress, new since Elizabeth's time, and accommodated in more civilized if also more austere fashion than her confrères at the men's colleges, informed her that all the women dons she had known were at present out of Oxford – berugged and befurred, Elizabeth supposed, in the sunlight of a Swiss hotel terrace, or sequestered in a quiet corner of the *Bibliothèque Nationale*, annotating with minute and unflagging industry the scribal errors of some medieval manuscript . . . Elizabeth turned away, disappointed. She had made up her mind, without any particular confidence, that what she needed was company and conversation – even the company and conversation of female dons. She found a telephone-box, and telephoned fruitlessly to acquaintances until her supply of pence was exhausted; considered renewing it at a nearby shop, and almost immediately lost heart; wandered morosely towards the Taylorian, half intending to look up a recent German volume on fingerprints; and eventually – as she had all along rather expected – went to a cinema.

The two films she saw did little to dissipate the cloud of depression which was gathering round her. The first was one of those documentaries, so dear to the critics of the Sunday press, about the Earth and those who lead their simple lives in constant contact with it. A sententious voice uttered a sententious and at times appalling commentary ('The life is the wheat, the red wheat, the white wheat; the wheat is the life', etc. etc.). There was a seemingly interminable sequence depicting a primitive childbirth. And the end of it all was an obscenely hygienic apocalyptic vision – the more progressive characters staring wet-eyed but optimistic into the Future – of almost everyone being inoculated against something or other; with, Elizabeth presumed (though the film made no mention of this), the usual crop of post-inoculation horrors so amiably set forth in the handbooks.

The second film concerned spies, and might perhaps have been considered as one of the lesser tolls levied on a peaceable and inoffensive world by Hitler's paranoia. It was one of those films in which, at the beginning, there is great uncertainty as to who is on what side, and in which, at the end, the problem has not been properly elucidated. Besides, this example was particularly odious in resorting to a gas whose sole and invariable potency lay in causing people to rise from their beds at dead of night and precipitate themselves, uttering loud and melancholy cries, over adjacent cliffs . . . Elizabeth left the cinema in a condition of black accidie, pausing only to inform an elderly gentleman who was on the point of buying a ticket that if he expected to be entertained by what he saw he had better think again. What action he took as a result of this advice, apart from raising his hat and mumbling unintelligibly, Elizabeth did not wait to observe.

There followed a prolonged and exhausting search for Virginia cigarettes. Clutching her sole *trouvaille* – twenty of an obscure and evidently obnoxious brand – Elizabeth returned, tired, cold, and irritable, to the hotel. It was just after half past four when she entered the foyer. In the public lounge on the left the tables were spread with white cloths, and a number of people were devouring an insubstantial and expensive tea. Joan Davis, descanting inexpertly upon the Shorthouse affair to Karl Wolzogen, caught sight of Elizabeth as she paused in the doorway, and signalled an invitation. Elizabeth crossed the room to join them.

'But I mustn't stay,' she said. 'Because I want some tea.'

Karl beamed; his enthusiasm was childlike and infectious. 'But you must stay, Mrs Langley, and take tea with us. Of course you must.' He turned to Joan. 'Did I not say? What an Octavian to your Marschallin! Has she not the perfect figure for it?' He surveyed Elizabeth from head to foot, with the most inoffensive frankness and admiration.

But Elizabeth, though cheered by this reference to her figure, was adamant on the subject of tea.

'If you'll forgive me,' she said. 'I'll have it in my room. For one thing, I want to change, and for another, they take so long to serve it down here.'

Karl was crestfallen. '*Ganz wahr*,' he admitted. 'But I will hurry the man. You will see. I shall say to him, is it right that the friend of a man who has seen Wagner in Bayreuth should wait for her tea? And he will say: of course not! I will bring it at once!'

'Really, you know' said Joan kindly, 'I don't think the waiter would even know who Wagner was.'

'Not know of Wagner?' Karl was aghast. 'But this is unbelievable . . .' He paused for a moment, focusing this new and dreadful revelation; then he groaned resignedly. 'Ah you English! It is as your poet Arnold has said: you are Philistines.' He sat down abruptly, and then, seeing that Elizabeth was still standing, scrambled hastily to his feet again. 'Consider,' he added by way of illustration, 'the lodgings where I stay.'

'Karl finds his lodgings unendurable,' Joan explained.

'*Ach, ja.*' Karl nodded sombrely. 'They are all lace and

smells and – what do you call them? – green things in great glazed pots.'

'Aspidistras?'

'*Ja, gewiss*. But it cannot be helped. It is due, you see, to the shortage of lodgings on the part of Oxford and the shortage of money on the part of me.'

'What I really want to know,' said Elizabeth, 'is whether there are any more developments in the Shorthouse business?'

'He is dead,' said Karl with finality, 'and that is a great blessing to us all. We will hope that the murderer is not discovered.'

'I hardly think I should take that attitude with the police,' remarked Joan a little faintly, 'if I were you . . . But really, Elizabeth, I should have thought you would have known about developments if anyone did. You seem to have been in the thick of it. I've heard virtually nothing, except that some people seem to think it was suicide . . .'

'It wasn't, though,' said Elizabeth. 'Unless,' she added after a pause, 'it was suicide arranged so as to look like murder. Such things have happened . . . But I admit it scarcely seems likely in Edwin's case.'

'Have you any theories?' Joan asked. 'After all, you're an expert on these affairs.'

'Theories? Well . . . I suppose I have, in a way.' Elizabeth frowned slightly. 'In fact, I think I know who was responsible.'

Joan stared at her. 'You *know* . . . But, my dear girl, have you told the police?'

'N-no. Not yet. I haven't told anybody. I haven't got enough proof so far.'

'You wouldn't consider taking us into your confidence?'

Smiling, Elizabeth shook her head. 'I'm terribly sorry . . . Perhaps later. In any case, it's just possible I'm wrong.'

'What a girl,' said Joan resignedly. 'Well, I suppose we shall have to possess our souls in patience.' A new thought occurred to her. 'Of course, if you really *do* know, Elizabeth, you ought to be forcibly silenced. You mustn't go about sending public benefactors to the gallows.'

Elizabeth laughed. 'I never realized murder was a benefaction . . . By the way, what's happening about the production?' She stepped out of the way of a hastening waiter.

'George Green is coming to sing Sachs. He hasn't got Edwin's voice, but he's a better actor. I gather they're hoping not to postpone the opening night. George knows his stuff, and he's prepared to work hard . . . Incidentally, what have you done with Adam?'

'He's gone to Amersham to see Charles Shorthouse.'

'*How* nice of him,' said Joan dreamily. 'I hope he gets past Beatrix. *A Night-Hag riding through the air to dance with Lapland Witches* . . . However' – she roused herself from this Miltonic reverie – 'there's going to be a rehearsal this evening, so I hope he doesn't stay away too long.'

'I don't think it occurred to him that there could possibly be one today,' said Elizabeth.

'Well, George Green has *arrived*, you see. And apparently the police have given us permission to use the theatre.'

Elizabeth became conscious that time was passing and that Karl, still courteously on his feet, was becoming a trifle restive.

'I must go,' she said. 'Thanks for the invitation, and my apologies for refusing it.'

'My dear, I quite understand. There are times when one just doesn't want to be sociable.'

Elizabeth smiled and left them.

* * *

At this point a discouraging admission has to be made – namely, that Elizabeth had, as a matter of fact, only the vaguest and most irrational of notions as to the identity of Edwin Shorthouse's murderer; nor was she by any means as certain as she had made out that the answer was not, after all, suicide. She had succumbed for a moment, while talking to Joan and Karl, to a craving for effect, and she blushed, bit her lip, and cursed herself roundly as she walked away. 'Really, how childish,' she thought. 'I deserve to be spanked. I'm a scatter-brained, pretentious little idiot . . .' Her depression returned. It was true that she was inclined to be suspicious of Boris Stapleton, but she knew perfectly well that she had no serious grounds for this whatever, and to have degenerated into vain and silly chatter on the subject angered her immeasurably. 'I deserve,' she repeated firmly to herself, 'to be beaten very severely indeed.'

She interviewed the head waiter, to ensure that in the future no strangers should share her table; a garrulous fellow had bored her all through lunch, and she was determined that this should not happen again. The head waiter received her orders with that sneering deference in which head waiters excel. Elizabeth suffered a further diminution of self-confidence. She entered the hotel lift in a mood compounded equally of abasement and fury.

The double room which she occupied with Adam was situated on the second floor of the hotel, and had a private bathroom attached. Before going in, Elizabeth found a chambermaid and ordered tea. Then she slammed the door behind her, took off her coat, flung her bag on to the dressing-table, and slumped down on one of the beds. Contemplating the impersonal neatness and comfort which surrounded her, she decided that the best remedy for her present mood would be a hot bath. After a while she undressed, slipped on a white silk wrap, and went into the bathroom. She did not pause to observe that the bedroom door had reacted unfavourably to *force majeure* and was not properly latched. As she was bending to turn on the taps, three things happened at once.

The telephone bell began to ring.

Elizabeth half-heard, half-felt, a stealthy movement behind her, and the next instant her neck was in the clutch of hard, efficient fingers.

And there came a knocking on the bedroom door.

Elizabeth fainted. All she afterwards remembered was a kind of helpless rage at her own inability to scream or to struggle, and at the appalling moral disadvantage which her scanty clothing implied. Blackness invaded her mind an instant before she crumpled up on the floor.

When she recovered consciousness, the first thing she did was to look at her watch, she had been lying there, she supposed, for five or ten minutes . . . And again there was a knocking on the bedroom door.

She got slowly and unsteadily to her feet, tenderly caressing the fading red finger-marks on her neck. She adjusted the wrap, which had partly fallen away from her body. Then she went slowly out into the empty bedroom.

She called: 'Who – who's there?' and was unable to suppress the trembling of her voice.

'Your tea, madam.'

'I – all right. I'm coming.'

She opened the door. The chambermaid brought in her tray, set it on a table, hesitated.

'Excuse me, madam, but – aren't you well?'

Elizabeth tried to smile. 'I'm all right,' she said. 'Thanks very much.' She felt dizzy again, and sat down quickly. A thought struck her.

'Did you – have you seen anyone leave this room during the last few minutes?'

The chambermaid was elderly, and anxious to help.

'Why, yes, madam – just as I was coming along the passage. A tallish lady, fair, wearing a navy-blue coat and skirt and a Fair Isle jumper. She *did* seem in a hurry.'

'I – I see. Thank you.'

'Isn't there anything I can do for you, madam?' said the chambermaid, and added, in an access of motherly warmth: 'You look that shaky, truly you do.'

'No, really, thanks.' Elizabeth tried again to smile, and this time succeeded. 'I just felt a little faint. I'm quite recovered now.'

When the chambermaid had gone, she was careful to see that this time the door was properly closed (it was of the kind which can be opened from the outside only with a key). It did not at the moment occur to her that the person who had attacked her might be still in the room – hidden, perhaps, in the tall and roomy wardrobe – and with more subtle resources at his or her disposal.

'*A tallish lady, fair . . .*' Evidently it had been Joan Davis. But, equally evidently, her visit might have had some perfectly innocent object. A scribbled note, discovered on the dressing-table, suggested as much. '*Door open,*' it ran, '*so I walked in. I forgot to say that the rehearsal's due to start at 5, though I don't expect many people will be on time. Will you tell Adam when he gets back?*' It was reasonable enough. Since Elizabeth had been lying quiet and unconscious in the bathroom, Joan might well have thought there was no one about. And yet . . .

Crumpling the note absent-mindedly in the palm of her left hand, Elizabeth returned to the bathroom and washed. Beneath the hum of the traffic in George Street she did not hear the brief, stealthy activity in the bedroom behind her, or the faint click of the outer door as it opened and closed again. Back in the bedroom, she dressed, did her hair and applied lipstick with a methodical deliberation half consciously directed against the horror which seemed to be creeping into her very bones. The tea-things appeared undisturbed. With a hand that shook a little, Elizabeth poured out a cup of tea and raised it to her lips.

Chapter Twelve

On their way back, Fen and Adam stopped in High Wycombe to get the wing of the car repaired. The garage-men, as is the way of garage-men, grizzled and grumbled and shook their heads over it, and diagnosed a number of other mechanical defects hitherto unsuspected; but Fen would have none of this, and prodded them so effectively that in half an hour, which they occupied in getting some tea, they were on the road again.

'All the same,' said Adam, resuming an argument which had been interrupted by this interlude, 'you can't tell me Charles Shorthouse is as naïve as all that. He's far from being stupid, you know.'

'I'm aware of that. All I maintain is that he's intelligent exclusively *in his own department*. As a general rule, composers aren't the brightest of mortals, except where music's concerned. And not always about music, either. You remember Tchaikovsky couldn't see anything in Brahms, Wagner, or any of his contemporaries except Bizet. No, it seems to me quite credible that Charles Shorthouse should have solemnly mugged up a lot of stuff about criminology as soon as he decided to murder his brother. I admit' – Fen was fiddling with the choke; Lily Christine jerked and spat horribly – 'I admit that one could scarcely be taken in by that wide-eyed, innocent narrative about last night . . .'

'You mean it wasn't true?'

'No. I don't mean that. It may very well have been true. All I mean is that Shorthouse must have known that his presence in Oxford would pretty soon be discovered, and was taking the precaution of telling us all about it in advance. It's suspicious, evidently, if people just don't mention these things at all.'

'But if he wanted to divert suspicion, why tell us that he was intending to kill his brother?'

'Possibly a kind of sophisticated bluff. But I'm not at all sure, you know, that that isn't what he *did* intend to do. I really wouldn't put it past him. In fact, I believe he'd be completely ruthless where his own works were concerned, and sacrifice anything or anybody to getting them done. He's a monomaniac – but then, most geniuses are. Look at Wagner . . . The problem, really, is not whether he *intended* to kill his brother but whether he actually *did*.'

'We shall have to find that man at the "Mace and Sceptre" and check up on his movements.'

'Yes. Wilkes. We may as well do that as soon as we get in. You're staying there yourself, aren't you?'

Adam nodded, his hand straying towards the brake as they approached a dangerous crossroads.

'I'm interested,' Fen resumed after a moment's rare attention to the other traffic on the road, 'to hear that Charles Shorthouse and the Thorn woman got separated at some stage. Don't you think she's capable of committing murder to further his interests?'

Adam considered. 'Would she have the strength to string up a lump of suet like Edwin Shorthouse?'

'I don't know,' said Fen uneasily, 'but it isn't a possibility one can rule out. And then I can't see how the thing was done . . . I thought I had an idea, but it becomes less and less plausible the more I think about it.' He seemed depressed. 'Anyway, we now know why Edwin Shorthouse was in his dressing-room at that time of night.'

'Do we?' said Adam thoughtfully. 'I was wondering if there wasn't a simpler explanation.'

'Oh?'

'Something of the same sort happened before – about two years ago, when we were doing *Falstaff* at Cambridge. Edwin had rooms with a landlady who disapproved of drink, and he was obliged to keep his supplies at the theatre. History may be repeating itself.'

'We'll inquire,' said Fen. 'And we may as well do it on the way back. Where *was* he staying?'

'In Holywell. I can't remember the number, but I think I can recognize the place when we get there.'

'I should have thought a man in his position could have afforded to stay at a hotel.'

'He could afford it all right, but he was too mean.'

'What a symposium of deadly sins the poor fellow seems to have been . . . Afterwards,' said Fen, 'I must see Peacock. And I should like to have a talk with Joan Davis about Stapleton and that girl. Women have an instinct for the truth in such cases.'

They crossed Magdalen Bridge at a quarter past five, and drove to Holywell. Adam's theory about Edwin Shorthouse's landlady proved to be correct. She was a large, doleful, indistinct woman with a streak of cheerless religiosity, a tendency to misquote the Bible and an ample, if rather generalized, store of information on the destination of the soul after death. They understood that she had had no very high opinion of her late lodger and was in no doubt as to his present whereabouts. Strong drink, she added in response to persistent queries, had never been allowed to enter her house, being in her opinion contrary to godliness and the Christian religion. Unfortunately this assertion moved Fen to initiate a long and unprofitable argument about the marriage at Cana, and it was some minutes before they were able to get away.

'But you were quite right,' said Fen as they drove up Broad Street. 'And that, thank God, is one problem out of the way.'

'How are you going to find this man Wilkes?'

'Search the bars,' said Fen without hesitation.

'You know him well?'

'Only too well. He's a deaf and very aged colleague of mine at St Christopher's. And he's dishonest,' said Fen aggrievedly. 'He steals my whisky.'

They reached the 'Mace and Sceptre', and, pursued by a savage explosion from Lily Christine ('There it goes again,' said Fen complacently) pushed their way through the revolving doors and into the public lounge, where they were fortunate enough to find Wilkes waiting expectantly for opening time. Fen introduced him to Adam.

'Now, listen, Wilkes,' he went on without more preliminary, 'we want to know about Charles Shorthouse. The composer. It seems you were with him last night.'

'What's it got to do with you who I was with?' said Wilkes testily. 'Heh. Interfering busybody—'

'A man has been murdered—'

'Pity it wasn't you.'

'A man has been murdered, and I'm trying to find out who was responsible . . . As you see,' Fen explained to Adam,

'Wilkes is very old, and I fancy his mind is going . . . Well, Wilkes, were you with Charles Shorthouse or weren't you?'

'Can't hear a word you're saying.'

'Were you with Charles Shorthouse last night?'

'Yes.' The aged Wilkes spoke more soberly, though there was still a malignant gleam in his alligator eye. 'And with his succubus.'

'His succubus?' Fen was startled.

'Thorn.' Wilkes spoke emphatically and clearly, as though addressing himself to rather a slow understanding. 'The name is Thorn. A small, hyena-like woman.'

'Ah.'

'We drank coffee together,' said Wilkes dreamily. 'I imagine they arrived at half past ten. Then at eleven they suddenly made off.'

'Made off?'

'That's what I said,' said Wilkes. 'Heh. They made off. In pursuance, I imagined, of some bodily necessity.' He lingered over the delicate obliquity of this statement. 'But on reflexion,' he continued reluctantly, 'I don't think that can have been the reason. For one thing, they weren't back until half past eleven.'

'They left, and came back, together?'

Wilkes assented, with a regal nod.

'And didn't they give any explanation of their absence?'

'Now let me see.' Wilkes' gaze wandered about the lounge, seeming to seek inspiration in its mock-Tudor fireplace and leather-covered armchairs. 'Yes. Now I remember. Shorthouse explained to me, in confidence, that he was intending to kill his brother.'

Fen moved convulsively, and upset an ash-tray into his lap.

'Really,' he grumbled, brushing himself disjointedly, 'that is the limit . . . I presume you didn't take this seriously?'

'On the whole, no.' Wilkes began to display interest. 'But *did* he, in fact . . .?'

'Someone did.'

'Well, I never,' said Wilkes.

'Charles Shorthouse and the Thorn woman,' said Adam, 'have no alibi, then?'

'No. Nor has Stapleton. Nor has Judith Haynes.' Fen blew his nose with a trumpeting sound. 'Well, there's nothing to be gained from sitting here.' He got to his feet.

'Where are you going now?' Wilkes demanded.

'I shan't tell you,' said Fen offensively, 'because if I did you'd come tagging along behind. You were quite enough of a nuisance during that toyshop business. You stole a bicycle,' he added reproachfully.

'Heh,' said Wilkes, pleased. 'So I did. For two pins I'd steal another.'

'You stay here and get quietly drunk.'

'By the way,' said Wilkes. 'I found that whisky you'd hidden behind your books.'

Fen stared at him in exasperation. 'Really, Wilkes, I hope you didn't take it. You don't seem to realize how difficult it is to get.'

'It isn't difficult to get,' Wilkes pointed out, 'when one has access to *your* rooms.'

'You must put it back at once, Wilkes.'

'Can't hear you.'

'I said, *thief*.'

'Yes,' said Wilkes thoughtfully, 'the wind's bitter. I shouldn't be surprised if we had a really heavy fall of snow.'

They left him. In the entrance hall they were met by a page-boy with a message for Adam.

'Good Lord,' Adam exclaimed in dismay after reading it, 'they're having a rehearsal and they want to know why I'm not there.' He looked at his watch. 'I'm a bit late, but I suppose I can still get to some of it . . . Oh, blast.'

'Where is your wife, one wonders?'

'Somewhere about, I expect. I'd better try and get hold of her before I go off to the theatre.' Adam went to the reception desk. 'The key of room 72, please.'

'I think Mrs Langley took it, sir, about an hour ago.'

'I imagine she's upstairs,' said Adam, rejoining Fen.

They took the lift, and walked along a passage prolific of giggling chambermaids to room 72. Adam knocked. For a moment there was no reply.

'Odd,' he said. 'I suppose she must have gone off somewhere with the key.' He knocked again.

Then there was a small movement on the other side of the door, and they heard Elizabeth say in a low voice:

'Who is it?'

'It's me, darling. Adam.'

'Have you got someone with you?'

'Only Professor Fen. Are you undressed, or something?'

The door opened, and Elizabeth stood in the gap. She was pale, and breathing quickly, and she looked very young and defenceless. She said:

'Oh . . . Adam . . .'

He took her in his arms. 'My dear, what is it?'

She attempted to smile. 'It's just – ignoble panic,' she said, and they realized that she was very near to tears. 'You see – someone's been trying to poison me.'

107

Chapter Thirteen

The room was as undistinguished as most hotel bedrooms, with its discreet printed injunctions, its elaborate apparatus of blinds and curtains, and its multiplicity of lights: and though Adam and Elizabeth had been there long enough to impress a certain amount of character on its blankness, it remained at bottom obstinately functional. Fen settled in an armchair, after casting his hat inaccurately at a hook on the door, and offered them cigarettes.

'Well?' he queried.

'Aconitine,' said Elizabeth briefly. 'In the tea.'

They all looked at the tray. There was a full cup on it, now almost cold.

'How do you know?' said Fen.

'It comes of poring over these things. I held a little in my mouth, and it made my lips go numb.'

'You must have had some reason for suspecting.'

'Suspecting,' Elizabeth repeated wryly. Her big eyes, with their uneven, sardonic brows, were very grave. 'Yes. I had reason enough. You see—'

She went on to narrate, in detail, the events of the afternoon.

'So you can understand,' she concluded, 'just why I began

to have doubts about the tea.' She gestured apologetically. 'When one's studying these things, one gets cagey – just as medical students tend to credit themselves with having the diseases they're working on. At all events, I tried the stuff and' – she shrugged – 'that's all. Except that I decided I wasn't going to budge from here until Adam came back.'

Adam took her hand and pressed it gently. They were neither of them demonstrative persons, and there was much that they could afford to leave unsaid.

'Well, Gervase, what's the answer?' Adam demanded.

'The answer' – Fen was unusually pensive – 'would seem to be that someone is becoming very frightened indeed . . . What time did all this happen?'

'Between half past four and five.'

'I see.' Fen rose, crossed to the tea-tray, and picked up the cup. 'I think I'll try this,' he said, 'so as to be sure you're not mistaken.'

'Be careful,' Adam warned, joining him.

'Well, don't buffet me about,' Fen complained, 'while I'm putting it into my mouth. I don't want to appear prematurely at the judgement seat.'

He sipped apprehensively – and almost immediately fled into the bathroom, whence he reappeared accompanied by a strong smell of disinfectant.

'Yes, you were quite right,' he announced. 'Of course, it *might* be veratrine, but that's rather rare. Aconite's the obvious answer. We'll have to get the tea tested, though as far as I can remember it takes several days.'

'Stas-Otto process,' Elizabeth supplied competently.

'Would the aconite be difficult to get?' inquired Adam, whose ideas on toxicology were primitive to the point of superstition.

'You go out into the fields and hedgerows,' Fen conde-scended to explain, 'and dig up some monkshood. Then you dry the roots and powder them . . . *Et voilà*.' He began to prowl restlessly about the room. 'It would seem,' he said, 'that the motive for this attack lay in your rash remarks about knowing the murderer's identity. And yet' – he stopped pacing abruptly – 'and yet a completely unsupported assertion like that oughtn't to have caused such undue alarm.' He shook his head. 'You know, it really doesn't constitute an adequate motive at all. I'm wondering if there isn't some damning fact you've got hold of without being aware of it . . . No, I don't see that we can get any sort of help from the motive.' He began to walk about again, fidgeting as he went with the handles of drawers and cupboards. 'Let me get this clear; a moment before you were attacked you heard someone knocking on the door?'

Elizabeth assented. Fen continued on his orbit.

'I wonder who that was,' he said. 'The probability would be that it was Joan Davis, of course. One assumes that your attacker was alarmed by the knocking and concealed him or herself somewhere while Joan came in and left the note. Then . . . what happens then?'

'He's about to come out of his hiding-place,' said Adam, 'when the chambermaid arrives with the tea. After she's gone, Elizabeth shuts the door and returns to the bathroom. Our X creeps from hiding, pops the aconite in the tea, lets himself out, and vanishes.'

'Yes, I see,' said Elizabeth. 'And that means that it certainly can't have been Joan who tried to poison me. On the other hand—'

'On the other hand,' Fen interposed, 'it *could* have been

she who tried to strangle you. In that case the knocking may well have been due to the person who wanted to poison . . .'

'You don't really mean' – Elizabeth was plaintive – 'that you think *two* people were trying to finish me off?'

'I agree,' said Fen, 'that it is rather an *embarras de richesses*. But then' – he became aggrieved – 'this bedroom seems to have been about as populous as Piccadilly tube station, and there is just the possibility—'

Adam interrupted. 'I think,' he said, 'that our first reconstruction must be the right one. When all's said and done it's very unlikely that Joan killed Edwin Shorthouse. I admit she disliked him in a general way – who didn't? – but he wasn't *specifically* a nuisance to *her*. And if, as one imagines, Edwin's death and this business this afternoon are connected—'

It was Fen's turn to interrupt. 'If they're connected. I'm not saying they aren't, mind you. But it is, I suppose, possible that Joan Davis had some entirely independent grudge against Elizabeth.'

Adam snorted. 'No, no, that's absurd.'

'She wasn't, for example, in love with you, Adam?'

'Good God, no.'

'You mightn't yourself have perceived the fact.'

'No,' said Elizabeth. 'But *I* certainly should have done. You can really count that out, Professor Fen.'

Fen paused to gaze gloomily out of the window at the uncompromising brick façade of the New Theatre. 'Did you happen to notice,' he asked, 'if the person who attacked you was wearing gloves?'

'Yes,' said Elizabeth promptly. 'Quite definitely, yes.'

Fen went to the wardrobe and peered cautiously inside. He then disappeared into it, closing the door behind him. After a few moments he reappeared, awkwardly disentangling himself from Elizabeth's dresses and swearing quietly to himself. He made as if to examine the floor of the wardrobe, and then lost heart and abandoned the attempt. He gazed perfunctorily under the beds.

'A friend of mine,' he said thoughtfully, 'has his chamberpots fitted with musical boxes which come into operation when they're lifted from the floor. It embarrasses his guests greatly ... As to what we do now' – he scratched his head, by no means improving the natural unruliness of his hair – 'I think really that we'd better find out whether any of these comings and goings were observed. And we *must* see Joan Davis. If it was she who knocked on the door, she may well have had a glimpse of anyone who came along here in front of her.'

'She'll be at the rehearsal by now,' said Adam. 'And that's where I ought to be, too.'

Fen lit another cigarette; plainly he was worried.

'Look here, Elizabeth,' he said, 'until this business is cleared up you mustn't be alone – at any time. We'd better all go along to the rehearsal together.'

They began wrapping themselves up against the cold.

'By the way,' said Elizabeth, 'you never told me what came of your visit to Amersham.'

'Nothing to speak of.' Fen acquainted her with the indefinite results of their interviews with Charles Shorthouse and with Wilkes. 'It's simply a question,' he concluded, 'of whether, in this respect, Shorthouse is genuinely eccentric, or whether it's just a bluff.'

'He's eccentric normally,' Adam pointed out.

'Yes. But no doubt he's aware of the fact, and he may be trading on it. After all, his tale's so unlikely that *on the face of it* no one but a dolt would have invented it in self-defence ... Well, are we all ready?'

112

They locked the door, and in the corridor outside Fen pounced on a passing chambermaid.

'And where have you been all afternoon, my girl?' he demanded with Rhadamanthine severity.

'Ooh,' said the chambermaid, alarmed. She was young, with popping eyes and straight, straw-coloured hair. 'I 'aven't done nothing, sir.'

'I didn't ask you whether you'd *done* anything,' said Fen, peeved. 'I simply want to know if you were anywhere about here between half past four and five this afternoon.'

'Nothing's bin took, 'as it, sir?' The girl was open-mouthed with dismay.

'Took?' Fen applied himself laboriously to the elucidation of this remark, and then, finding the effort too much, abruptly abandoned it. 'Did you or did you not see anyone go into or come out of room 72 between those times?'

'Because if it 'as, you ought to tell the manager.'

'If it 'as what?' said Fen, disconcerted. 'The girl's a half-wit.'

What at last emerged from a good deal of tedious inquisition was unhelpful. It appeared that at half past four the chambermaids were in the habit of assembling in their sitting-room to brew tea; consequently none of them had been in the corridor, or within sight of it, at the crucial time.

'Except Effie,' added the victim of their inquiries after a pause for reflexion. 'She 'ad to take someone a tray. But as I say, sir, if anything's gorn . . .'

The significance of these recurrent utterances had at last penetrated to Fen's understanding. He became irresponsible.

'There's a diamond tiara gone,' he said sternly. 'And the specifications of the atomic bomb. So if we're all reduced to molecular dust before we have time to turn round it will be your fault.'

'Oh, sir,' said the chambermaid. 'You're 'aving me on.'

'You just wait and see,' said Fen, wagging his forefinger at her, 'you just wait and see if I'm having you on or not.' He departed, with Adam and Elizabeth, in search of Effie.

But here again they were unsuccessful; apart from Joan Davis, Effie had seen no one, either on her way to room 72 with Elizabeth's tea, or subsequently. Fen ascertained that the poison could not have been introduced into the tea before it arrived at the bedroom, and left it at that.

'Ye gods,' he exclaimed gloomily as they stood in the entrance hall. 'Or to crib a phrase from my illustrious colleague at the War Office – burn me. What other lines of approach are there?' He considered. 'Whereabouts in the hotel are the rooms of the other people connected with the opera?'

'Peacock's a few doors along the corridor from us,' said Adam. 'And Joan's on the floor above and John Barfield's on the floor below, I *think*. But we can look at the board.'

They went to the porter's box and studied the names and room-numbers displayed beside it.

'Yes,' said Adam. 'First floor.'

'What's more,' Fen put in, 'this wretchedly informative device ensures that no one needed to *ask* for your room number – which might have given us some kind of clue . . . Well, I'd better go to the manager and make sure those tea-things aren't taken away.'

'What about informing the police?'

'Mudge may be at the theatre. If not, we'll ring him up from there. We shall have to find out now where our sundry suspects were just before five.'

'It lets out Charles Shorthouse and the Thorn woman, doesn't it?'

'No, I don't think so. Remember that we delayed about half an hour in Wycombe to get Lily Christine mended, and that there's an alternative route to Oxford through Amersham and Missenden and Aylesbury. They could have got here well before us . . . Ridley,' he called to the porter, 'do you know Mr Charles Shorthouse by sight?'

Ridley, a thin, competent-looking elderly man in blue and braid, made negative gestures. 'I think not, sir. Mr Edwin Shorthouse – yes.'

Fen sighed. 'You see? Of course the waiter who served them last night may have seen him come in this afternoon . . . Ridley, is the waiter who was serving in the lounge after ten-thirty last night anywhere about?'

The porter consulted some kind of roster. 'McNeill. I'm afraid not, sir. It's his afternoon off today. He'll be at the cinema.'

'Oh, my dear paws,' said Fen in disgust. 'I suppose in that case there's nothing more we can do for the moment. I'll just look in on the manager, and then we can go.'

Chapter Fourteen

The rehearsal, when they reached it, was in a state of confusion which really amounted to total deadlock. It had been called, rather suddenly, for five o'clock; and since most of those concerned had assumed that there would be no rehearsal that day, and had gone out in search of such merriment as Oxford affords on a week-day afternoon, there were considerable gaps in the ranks, and it was difficult to do any useful work. However, the new Sachs had arrived with remarkable promptness – he was a competent singer whom Adam knew and liked – and Rutherston, in the absence of about a third of the orchestra, was taking him through moves. The remaining two-thirds of the orchestra, along with the chorus and one or two of the principals, pottered funereally about engaged in muted execration of Peacock, who had declined to let them go home on the grounds that the remainder of the cast and of the orchestra might yet appear, and so enable them to do at least an hour's work. Adam thought that on the whole he was justified, in view of the fact that the performance was due in less than a week's time.

There were few lights in the auditorium, though it was possible to make out the coffered ceiling and the white balcony with the illuminated clock set in its centre. On either side there was one tier of boxes, almost antiseptically severe in design, with blue velvet curtains and concealed lighting; while on the carved shield above the proscenium-arch two symbolic young women were sprawled, scantily clad, lubriciously curved, and holding slender angelic trumpets to their lips. ('They represent,' said Fen, 'the proctorial authority, summoning the youth of Oxford to virtue and sobriety.') On the stage, Rutherston could be heard complaining to George Green about the demeanour of the apprentices in the brawl at the end of the second act. 'They scamper about,' he said, 'like a herd of deer attacked by a Pekingese.' In the orchestra-pit, a trombonist was doing a very creditable imitation of a Spitfire diving, and a clarinettist was surreptitiously playing jazz. John Barfield was seated in the front row of the stalls, consuming a large orange.

Adam went to make his apologies to Peacock, whom he found talking to Mr Levi in the wings. Mr Levi was a large, kindly, polyglot Jew, with a powerful if somewhat inaccurate command of the English language.

''Allo, Langley,' he said. 'Terrible 'old-up, this. *Schrecklich, gar fabelhaft.* I tell you, I 'ave no use for that twister someone knock-off, see, but 'e 'ad a voice, nothing like it since Chaliapin, *famos, nicht wahr*? And now,' said Mr Levi with some relish, ''is tonsils'll be dinner for coffin-worms' sarcophaguses, clever little insects.'

Adam introduced him to Fen.

'Still,' Mr Levi resumed cheerfully, 'we get the show on none the less.' He patted Peacock encouragingly on the back. 'The maestro 'ere, 'e's good. I tell you – 'e keep that orchestra right where 'e want 'em. The 'ornplayers' – Mr Levi here became suddenly lyrical with enthusiasm, and addressed himself, gesticulating illustratively, to Fen – 'The 'orn-players, even, they listen to what 'e say and stop shaking the spit out of their 'orns, ain't it?'

Peacock assented confusedly to this doubtful recommendation.

'And *nicht nur das*,' said Mr Levi. 'Not only the 'orns, but the double-basses. You know 'ow it is with double-basses. They wink and snigger. It's the dames,' he explained to Elizabeth, 'what makes 'em wink and snigger. I tell you, I seen double-basses behave in a public concert like in a way would 'ave made me old mother blench, but it's all the same nowadays, it's *Vénus toute entiére à sa proie attachée*, the dames themselves is to blame for 'alf of it.'

Having delivered himself of this sentiment, Mr Levi left to return to London, after warmly wishing them all good luck and assuring them of his continued enthusiasm for the production. A few newcomers drifted in and uttered reluctant apologies to Peacock. The tuba-player arrived, unpacked his instrument, and began making a sound like a fog-horn on it, while the rest of the orchestra chanted 'Peter Grimes!' in a quavering, distant falsetto.

'I think,' said Peacock as he contemplated this phenomenon, 'that perhaps we'd better start.'

There could be no doubt, thought Adam, that the death of Edwin Shorthouse was not much regretted by either Peacock or anyone else connected with the production. Adam said as much to Fen.

'I know,' said Fen. 'It seems positively indelicate to be trying to discover his murderer.'

Joan Davis had joined them and was regarding Fen quizzically. 'Then you've quite made up your minds it was murder?'

'*I* have. I'm not so sure about the police . . . Adam, intro-duce us.'

Adam hastened to do so.

'Your Marschallin was magnificent,' said Fen. 'As good as Lotte Lehmann.'

Joan laughed. 'I wish I thought so. It would have to be superlative if it was that . . .' Suddenly her voice changed. 'Professor Fen, I'm in a mess. I wonder if you can help me?'

'I'll try. As a matter of fact I've been wanting to have a talk with you. Can we go' – Fen stared gloomily about him – 'somewhere a bit quieter?'

'George,' said Joan, 'what will you do when you finally get going?'

'The assembly of the Masters,' Peacock replied, 'and the trial song.'

'Then you don't want me?'

'Not for the moment.'

'Come on,' said Joan. 'We'll go up to my dressing-room.'

Fen turned to Adam. 'Can you sing the trial song and keep an eye on Elizabeth as well?'

'Yes.'

'I shall be perfectly all right,' said Elizabeth.

'That,' said Fen in parting, 'is probably what Caesar told Calpurnia at the Ides of March. So don't go mooning off on your own.'

'"All right"?' said Joan, as the two of them climbed the stairs to the dressing-rooms. 'Why shouldn't Elizabeth be all right?'

'For a reason' – Fen was noncommittal – 'which I'll tell you about in a moment . . . I hope you aren't on the second floor. *Mon beau printemps*, as Mr Levi would probably remark, *a fait le saut par la fenêtre*. Is this it?'

'This,' Joan assured him, 'is it.' She unlocked the door of her dressing-room.

Physically it resembled that in which Edwin Shorthouse had met his end; but its atmosphere was entirely different, and Fen marvelled anew at the relative sensitivity of the sexes to their immediate surroundings. The difference appeared to lie – he became momentarily abstracted and analytical – in the feminine predilection for profusion and colour. Joan's dressing-room was not less untidy than that of Shorthouse – if anything it was more so. But it was crowded with clothes, cosmetics, books, photographs, telegrams, and the effect of these things was to give it a friendlier and more comfortable air than the corresponding male habitation, with its comparative drabness and austerity. Joan switched on the electric fire (in that bitter February it was much needed); they sat beside it and lit cigarettes; and Fen returned to the matter in hand.

'Well,' he said. 'What sort of a mess is this you're in?'

Joan smiled. 'I thought you would have known.'

'It's to do with the police, is it? No, I haven't seen Mudge since lunch-time. What has he been up to?'

'Among other things he's been questioning Karl and me. And I think he's developed a theory.'

Fen groaned. 'Go on.'

'One of the things he elicited from Karl was that yesterday evening, after dinner, several of us held a kind of emergency meeting. It was to discuss the situation that had arisen during the rehearsal, and to consider means of dealing with it. It didn't come to any conclusion – such meetings seldom do – except that Edwin's parents should never have met. But unfortunately I made rather a compromising remark.'

'Well?'

'I said: "It would be nice if we could poison him just a *little* – just so as to make him unable to sing".'

Fen attempted to blow a smoke-ring, and failed miserably. 'I begin to see.'

'The Inspector asked me if I *had* said that, and of course I couldn't deny it. The trouble is, of course, that though out of its context it sounds decidedly sinister, in fact it was just one of those careless, silly things one does say.'

'Exactly.' Fen was leaning forward to warm his hands at the fire. 'But by itself—'

'Worse is to come,' said Joan, and laughed a little shakily. 'It seems that Edwin's gin was doped with Nembutal – and the only person round here who possesses any Nembutal is me.'

Fen sat upright. Distantly, they heard the music of the first act begin. Rich, sonorous, and dignified, Barfield's voice called the roll of the Masters. '*Now to a trial as summoned hither, masters in council are come together . . .*' A trial, Fen thought: God alone knew what fantastic notions this Nembutal business had put into Mudge's head.

'I get it on a prescription, of course,' Joan went on. 'For insomnia. And I have – or rather I had – quite a lot of it.'

'The past tense?'

'Most of it's gone. Something like four hundred grains, in fact.'

'Gone from where?'

'From this room.'

'You've been keeping it here?'

'Yes. Purely by chance. I packed in rather a hurry, put it in my dressing-case, and forgot about it until I got out my make-up the other day. I've been sleeping well recently, and haven't needed it. For the same reason I didn't bother to take it to the hotel.'

'But you keep this room locked?'

'Not always. As I seldom leave anything valuable here, I sometimes don't bother.'

'Anyone could have snaffled the stuff, in fact?'

'If they'd known it was there.'

'And did anyone know?'

Joan smiled wryly. 'Half the company, no doubt. You know Adela Brent who's singing Magdalena?' And when Fen shook his head: 'Well, I told *her* it was here, and like most of us she gossips. *"Did you know that Joan kept Nembutal in her dressing-room?"'* Joan mimicked. *'"I always suspected her of taking drugs."'*

'Yes,' said Fen pensively. 'It's the sort of trivial scrap of information which does get about. There's no lead there.' He paused for a moment. 'But I presume Mudge doesn't suspect you of *actually murdering* Shorthouse?'

'No, I don't think it's as bad as that.' Joan drew deeply on her cigarette. 'I fancy – though he didn't say anything about it – that he believes Edwin committed suicide. But I also think he imagines I tried to *poison* Edwin, if only for the reason that the Nembutal in the gin doesn't fit in with his suicide hypothesis.'

'The motive for this being—'

'Altruistic concern about the production. Or' – Joan flushed a little – 'not-so-altruistic concern about George.'

'Who is George?'

'George Peacock . . . Professor Fen, what ought I to do?'

'Nothing,' said Fen decidedly.

'But I *must* do something; I can't let them go on thinking—'

'Let them think what they please, and console yourself by recalling the dreadful example of Mr Blenkinsop.'

'Mr Blenkinsop?'

'Mr Blenkinsop is my favourite tragi-comic figure in history. It came to Mr Blenkinsop' (Fen went on with a happy, faraway look in his pale blue eyes), 'in the days when locomotives were adumbrated but not yet made, that in the pattern as commonly proposed, and whose descendents waft us incompetently about nowadays, the wheels would slip on the rails and the vehicle consequently remain motionless. He therefore devoted a great deal of time, money, and trouble to inventing a locomotive with spiked wheels which would not be liable to this disadvantage . . . With the result that you see. Mr Blenkinsop is the *locus classicus* of misplaced foresight. And it would be just as absurd if you were to try to take action about Mudge's suspicions.' Fen stubbed out his cigarette and spoke more energetically. 'There isn't a shadow of a case against you, unless—' Fen broke off suddenly.

'Unless what?'

'Unless the jury brings in a charge of attempted murder or grievous bodily harm or something at the inquisition. That would be equivalent to an indictment – but of course it's wildly unlikely, and in any case the thing would never stand up for a moment in court.'

'In other words,' said Joan, 'I'm in a senseless panic . . . Well, well, one goes on learning things about oneself. And now, what was it *you* wanted to talk to *me* about?'

'A general inquisition, if I may.'

'Go ahead.'

'Tell me about Stapleton and Judith Haynes.'

Joan's shrewd, puckish face suggested that she was perturbed. 'What do you want to know? They're very much in love with one another. He composes. I was glancing through the vocal score of his opera after tea today.'

'Mudge delivered it up?'

'Yes, it was found in Edwin's rooms.'

'Is it a good opera?'

'Not really.' Joan grimaced. 'But he's quite young, of course, and some composers develop late. Anyway, it's not fair to judge it when one's head's full of *Meistersinger*. As Puccini said, we're all mandolin-twangers in comparison with Wagner. *Pace* W.J. Turner.'

'W. J. Turner,' said Fen dreamily, 'thinks *The Flying Dutchman* is Wagner's best opera.' He made trumpeting noises, vaguely reminiscent of the overture to that work. 'But as for *Meistersinger* – apart from *Henry IV* it's the only thing I know which convinces one of the essential nobility of *man*; as opposed to *Macbeth* and the Ninth Symphony, which are really about the gods . . .' He paused to listen to the distant strains of Pogner's Address, and then returned somewhat hurriedly to the matter in hand. 'But as regards Judith Haynes and Edwin Shorthouse—'

'Edwin?' In the flurry of the moment Joan spoke a little too casually. 'I think he had hopes of Judith. But his intentions weren't honourable, to say the very least of it.'

'What makes you say that?' Fen's eyes held a curious glitter, like those of a snake confronted by a particularly gullible and trusting rabbit.

'Oh, I – that's just the way Edwin was.'

'There wasn't any particular incident—'

'To be quite frank,' Joan interrupted him, 'I made a promise.'

'Then you'd better break it,' said Fen, leaning back in his chair. 'Unless of course there's something discreditable to these young people which you want to hide.'

'No . . . no. But still—'

'If I told you another person's life was in danger, would that make any difference?'

'Are you serious?'

'Perfectly.'

'But *they* can't have anything to do with it.'

'Probably not. But every scrap of evidence is important.'

Joan hesitated. Then: 'Well, here goes,' she said, 'for what it's worth . . . Edwin made some sort of attempt to rape Judith Haynes, when he was drunk. And Boris Stapleton heard about it.'

She explained. 'Poor Judith,' she said. ' "Clothing disarranged", as the Sunday papers put it. I don't think I've ever seen quite such misery and hatred in a human face – she's instinctively virginal, that child . . . Well, attacks like that haven't much chance of succeeding at the best of times, but of course I interfered.'

'What did you do?' Fen asked, interested.

'I got him by his coat collar and the seat of his pants,' said Joan with nostalgic pleasure. 'There must be something particularly disconcerting about that, because it seems to paralyse people . . . Then I tripped him, and he toppled down and banged his head.'

These amazonian tactics evidently pleased Fen. 'Most satisfactory,' he agreed. 'But how did Stapleton get to know of it?'

'Judith must have told him. He came to me the day afterwards, looking rather queer, and thanked me. But . . . well, there's no doubt he felt pretty strongly about it.' She paused, and as Fen said nothing: 'I suppose that adds to your list of motives?'

'Not appreciably,' said Fen. He was now frankly sprawling, his long legs stretched out towards the fire, his gold cigarette-case, temporarily forgotten, held in his right hand. 'It's only confirmation of what I already suspected. Now about your own movements last night . . .'

'Just as a matter of routine.'

'Exactly what I was going to say,' Fen remarked benevolently. He gave her a cigarette and put the case away again. 'Any alibi?'

'None whatever. Immediately after our meeting at the Randolph I walked back to the "Mace and Sceptre" and went to bed. That would be fairly soon after nine.'

'And thereafter you might at any time have crept out, disguised as an atom physicist and unobserved by anyone.'

'Yes. There are plenty of back exits from the hotel . . . As a matter of fact, though, I didn't.'

'No.' Fen spoke a little absent-mindedly. He produced a lighter and lit Joan's cigarette for her. 'Can you tell me what you've been doing since lunch today?'

'Yes, of course – but why?'

'There are reasons,' Fen assured her amicably. He reflected, as he spoke, that unfortunately no kind of trap was possible in inquiring about the attacks on Elizabeth. 'And quite good ones at that.'

'You make me nervous,' said Joan. 'Now I shall probably leave something out, or get my times mixed, and you'll have me carried off to gaol on suspicion of something.'

The warmth of the electric fire was making Fen sleepy. He roused himself and grinned at her. 'Think hard,' he said unconsolingly.

'Well . . . after a late lunch I went to the residents' lounge and wrote letters. There must be plenty of people who can guarantee I really was there. About four Karl turned up – I'd invited him to tea. He'd just spent a very hectic hour, poor dear, communicating with people about this rehearsal. We went to the public lounge. Then the Inspector arrived. We gave him a cup of tea, and he asked us questions.'

'Did you see or talk to anyone connected with the opera while you were having tea – apart from Wolzogen, that is?'

'No, I don't think – oh, yes, of course, Elizabeth. But only for a few minutes. That was after the Inspector had left.'

'What did you talk to her about?'

Joan frowned. 'Nothing special, I fancy. Just vague chatter.' A thought occurred to her. 'But haven't you spoken to Elizabeth? It seems she has some fairly definite idea about who did what to Edwin.'

'She *had* such an idea,' said Fen with great firmness. He still misdoubted this as a motive for the attacks on Elizabeth, but it might as well be quashed at the earliest possible opportunity. 'Since then it's been proved to be quite false.'

'I see . . . Shall I go on?'

'Please.'

'Karl left shortly after Elizabeth. I think he went upstairs to see George. I finished my tea, and then it occurred to me that we'd neither of us told Elizabeth what *time* the rehearsal was supposed to be. I thought I'd look in and remedy that, as she was up in her room . . . At least, that's where I imagined she was. Actually I found the door off the latch and no one there.'

The door off the latch . . . That suggested culpable carelessness on the part of Elizabeth's attacker, Fen thought: unless of course Joan had been that attacker, and was now lying to conceal the fact. He glanced covertly at her, and it came to him with something of a shock that potentially at least she might well be without scruples. Beneath her pervasive charm there was a certain hardness – though that in itself militated against her having been concerned in the

127

attacks on Elizabeth, which appeared to have been inadequately conceived and carried out in a state of something like panic.

'I was all the more surprised,' she was saying, 'because as I knocked I thought I heard some kind of movement inside the room. But I suppose it must have been next door.'

'You didn't look in the bathroom?'

'No-no. The door was partly open, but there wasn't any sound, so I didn't bother to investigate . . . Professor Fen, what is all this about? Does it concern Elizabeth?'

'Yes,' said Fen. 'It does. There were two attempts to kill her this afternoon, both about the time you went up to her room. Anonymous attempts, I should add. That's why your evidence may be important.'

'To *kill* her? But why? Why?' Joan had been startled out of her habitual equanimity.

Fen shrugged. 'We don't know. But go on. After you'd left the note—'

'The note?' Joan spoke confusedly. 'Oh, yes, of course. I just put on a coat and hat and came round here. That's all.'

'Now, try and remember, please.' Fen leaned forward. 'When you went up to that room, did you see anyone in front of you going in the same direction?'

Joan considered. 'No,' she answered at last. 'I'm pretty certain I didn't.'

Fen suppressed a sigh of disappointment, and fell to recalling the exact topography of the hotel corridor. There was a right-angle bend, he remembered, immediately before one arrived at room 72, so that in approaching from the stairs and lifts one would have to be right up to the door in order to see anyone enter it. Beyond the bend there were a few more bedrooms (among them that of Peacock); then lavatories and bathrooms; and at last the corridor resolved itself into a cul-de-sac, with nothing at the end but a wall, a frosted-glass window, and a radiator. Yet if Joan were telling the truth, the attacker must have come from the direction opposite to that of the stairs and the lifts. He might have been lurking previously in a bathroom or a lavatory – only there was no plausible reason why he should. And on the other hand, he might have come from Peacock's room . . .

Fen shook his head. The affair was exasperatingly elusive – the more so as Elizabeth's assailant had been sufficiently insouciant to give himself away ten times over. Nor, now he came to think of it, had this interview been very much help; its sole justification, in fact, lay in the dispiriting news that Mudge was developing theories of his own.

Fen got energetically to his feet, becoming once more aware of the distant music; aware, too, that Joan was regarding him curiously.

'Class dismissed?' she asked.

'With full marks,' he said. 'Now I must find someone else to pester. Are you staying here?'

'No. I'll come down, I think, and see what progress they're making.' Fen opened the door for her. 'Oh, damn,' she said. 'I haven't turned the fire off.'

Fen went back and turned it off for her.

'It stinks,' he said gravely, 'and I am ready to depart.'

Chapter Fifteen

'One of my happiest memories,' said Joan as they descended the stairs, 'is playing Salome in Strauss's opera with Edwin in the unlikely role of John the Baptist. It was some time ago, when I really had a figure' ('You have still,' Fen put in gallantly), 'and I remember it partly because I realized even then that I was the first Salome to give the males in the audience a really good run for their money during the Dance of the Seven Veils. It was at the Paris opera, and I ended up in a condition of nudity which would have made the Windmill girls blush . . . However, that wasn't what I was going to say. There stood Edwin, sternly resisting my charms, pudgy, half-naked, and with a corpulence barely credible in a man who'd lived so long on locusts and wild honey. And do you know' – Joan stopped abruptly in front of the door which led into the auditorium – 'do you know, I found him *revolting*. "*Let thy white body be touched by me*",' she quoted. 'And really, if I'd *had* to touch him, I think I should have screamed . . .'

'All this,' Fen suggested, 'being relevant to the attempted rape of Judith Haynes.'

'Yes. God knows *I'm* hard boiled enough, and that was on the stage. What *she* must have felt—'

They actually found Judith Haynes sitting with Elizabeth,

and went to join them. The rehearsal, it was evident, was going with a swing. Adam – who up to now had been playing the entire scene with his gaze fixed unwaveringly on his wife, to the great astonishment and dismay of Rutherston – was singing Walther's trial song. The first oboe had not even yet appeared, and Peacock, from the rostrum, periodically supplied his part by a hollow sepulchral chanting which greatly disconcerted everyone. Nonetheless, there was an atmosphere of good-humour about the proceedings now that things were fairly under way – and moreover, a greater air of plausibility than in any of the rehearsals so far. People were acting as well as singing; moves went smoothly; the scenery had crystallized into dim but still unmistakable simulacra of its ultimate forms. Joan realized that a weight had lifted from the production by the death of Edwin Shorthouse, and because she was a loyal member of her profession the realization made her happy.

She settled down beside Judith Haynes.

'Judith,' she said quietly, 'I'm afraid I've had to break my promise to you. I've told Professor Fen about what happened the other night.'

The girl turned, and Joan wondered if it was the artificial light or some unguessed-at private reason which made her pretty, youthful features seem momentarily haggard.

'It's all right,' she said. 'I've just been telling Mrs Langley, too. It doesn't matter now that Boris knows.'

Instantly she bit her lip and glanced swiftly at Fen. Elizabeth, moved to pity by her anxiety, hastened to break the small, embarrassed silence which followed.

'Edwin,' she stated, 'was entirely detestable.'

Something in the tone of her voice attracted Fen's attention. He looked at her with mild interest, through half-closed eyes.

'How long have you known Edwin Shorthouse?' he inquired.

'About as long as I've known Adam . . . We had a triangle,' Elizabeth explained; and then feeling perhaps that this curt geometrical comment might appear unmannerly, hastened to add: 'Edwin, you see, wanted me for his mistress . . . He wasn't at all pleased when Adam married me, and for some time he behaved atrociously.'

'Adam didn't like him, then?'

'Not so much that: *he* detested *Adam.*'

'"Detest" is a strong word,' said Fen.

'In this instance it's the only possible word.'

'Were they still at loggerheads when Shorthouse died?'

'No,' said Elizabeth. 'He apologized to Adam at the end of last year, when they were working together in *Don Pasquale.*' She gave Fen an account of the incident. 'Adam didn't seem to think the apology was genuine, but we had no more trouble subsequently.'

This information seemed obscurely to disappoint Fen. He looked back at the stage. Adam had finished the trial song, and Beckmesser was engaged, with all possible gusto, in pulling it to pieces. The Masters, with the exception of Sachs, shook their heads in disapproval of their Walther's youthful iconoclasm. A charwoman with mop and bucket peered interestedly out of the wings, and was ordered away by someone invisible behind her. And Judith said to Joan:

'I'm terribly worried about Boris.'

'Worried? Why?'

'I'm sure he's ill, and he simply won't see a doctor.'

'There's some sort of skin disease, isn't there?'

'Yes. He's had that before, but it's never made him as ill as this.'

132

'*Why* won't he see a doctor?'

'Because of the opera. It's his first part – only two words, I know, but still, his first part. He's afraid of being ordered to bed. And he's working so hard to make a career for himself – he practises make-up, you know, for an hour every day . . .'

'Do you think that if I spoke to him—'

'No . . . That is, I don't mean to be rude, but if *I* can't persuade him . . .'

'Yes. I quite see that.' Joan came suddenly to a decision. 'Come and talk to me privately.'

They went to the rehearsal-room. Giacomo Puccini eyed them beadily from the wall.

'Judith,' said Joan without more preliminary, 'are you living in sin with your young man?'

'I-I – no,' the girl stammered. 'That is to say—'

'Let me put it this way,' said Joan kindly. 'Have you ever been to bed with him?'

Judith's face was scarlet. 'No, I – I haven't. He's asked me to, but I was afraid—'

'That you'd have a baby. Very cautious and commendable. Why on earth don't you get married?'

Judith stared at Joan as though she had suggested a trip to the moon. 'M-married? But we couldn't afford it—'

'If you can afford to live separately you can afford to live together, provided you don't saddle yourselves with children straight off.'

'But – but my parents wouldn't want—'

'They'll get over it,' said Joan ruthlessly, 'when they find it's a *fait accompli*. Are you both over twenty-one?'

'Yes, but you see—'

'If I get you a special licence, will you be married at once?'

Judith no longer stammered. 'Yes,' she said simply.

133

'Good for you.' Joan smiled. 'Talk it over with Boris, and let me know. If you really think it would be unwise, don't do it. But if you're just being careful, stop being careful and be happy instead.'

Judith kissed her impulsively. They returned in silence to the others.

Act one was nearly at an end. Adam, with an angry gesture, left the stage. The Masters crowded out after him, jostled and buffeted by their apprentices. Sachs alone remained, while for three bars the orchestra recalled the trial song. Then he strode after the others, as the music swept on to its final F major chord. There was a general sigh of relaxation. The players began groping hopefully for their instrument cases; the cast drifted back into view.

'Thank you, ladies and gentlemen,' said Peacock. 'We'll leave it at that for this evening. I'm afraid this snap rehearsal has inconvenienced many of you, but I hope you'll forgive me, in view of the difficult circumstances and the nearness of opening night. I'm cancelling the rehearsal tomorrow morning because of the inquest, but I hope we may be able to resume in the afternoon on the old schedule as posted by the stage door. Thank you all very much.'

He disappeared into the well of the orchestra-pit and shortly came to join Elizabeth, Joan, Judith and Fen in the auditorium. His hair was tousled, he was sweating and exhausted, but he was nevertheless triumphant.

'It's pulling together,' he said to Joan. 'Didn't you think so?' She nodded, smiling a little at his excitement. 'George Green,' he went on, 'is God's own gift to a conductor. He seems to know what I want by sheer instinct. And the nuances Langley gets into the trial song . . . If he hadn't looked all the time as though he were seeing a ghost, it would have been perfect.'

'My dear,' said Joan warmly. Almost involuntarily she touched his hand with hers. He looked at her sharply for an instant, and then laughed.

'I'm very naïve, aren't I?' he said charmingly. 'I can't think how you all manage to put up with me.'

Adam and George Green arrived, and conversation became general. Fen, observing that it was concerned solely with operatic matters, took the opportunity of a word with Judith Haynes. For the opening of this brief interview he deliberately employed every resource of charm and tact he could muster, since he knew he must go warily.

'Just one question,' he said, 'if you'll allow me to be a nuisance . . .' And then he stopped, for he saw that Judith was happy – so happy as to make charm and tact a trifle redundant. He proceeded more boldly.

'Will you tell me,' he said, 'if you and Stapleton came to this rehearsal together?'

'If – if what?' She was hardly listening. Then she hurriedly collected her wits. 'Oh . . . I'm sorry. I don't know what's the matter with me. Would you mind saying that again?'

Fen repeated the question.

'Oh. No, we didn't. Boris went for a walk this afternoon and came here directly. He heard about the rehearsal from someone in the orchestra.'

'He was here when you arrived?'

'No, he came in a few minutes after me . . . Is that all?'

'That,' said Fen rather sombrely, 'is all.' *A walk*, he reflected: Stapleton's habit of going for a walk whenever some crux occurred was decidedly discouraging.

He went back with Adam, Elizabeth and Joan to the door of the 'Mace and Sceptre'. Before saying good night:

'Joan,' he asked, 'what was it you said to Judith?'

'I advised her to marry her young man at the earliest possible moment!'

Fen made no reply. Joan added with a touch of asperity: 'Don't you approve?'

'There's just this about it,' said Fen slowly, 'that we're up to our necks in a murder case, and it would be only an elementary precaution to avoid a decisive step of that kind until it's been solved.'

Elizabeth unexpectedly lost her temper. 'Don't you think, Professor Fen,' she snapped, 'that you're better qualified to get on and solve it than to offer silly advice about people's personal affairs?'

Fen answered without a trace of resentment. 'I don't think,' he said, 'that I'm very well qualified for anything . . . Well, I'll see you at the inquest. Good night, and sleep well.'

'Oh, Elizabeth,' said Adam sadly, 'I don't think you ought to have said that.'

Then they quarrelled. It was their first quarrel since marriage. For an hour they sulked, and at the end of an hour were rapturously reconciled. Adam got so drunk celebrating this latter event that they quarrelled again.

Chapter Sixteen

It was late on a Monday night that Edwin Shorthouse met his death; on the Tuesday afternoon Elizabeth was attacked; and the inquest was arranged for the Wednesday morning. An hour before it was due to begin, Fen arrived at the 'Mace and Sceptre' to see Peacock.

This, he hoped, would be the last interview necessary, apart perhaps from a few words with Karl Wolzogen; and he was obliged to admit to himself, as he entered the familiar foyer, that the progress he had made so far was uncommonly small. It had become gradually evident that the official theory could be summed up as suicide; Mudge had explained over the telephone that morning that he regarded the Nembutal in the gin bottle as unconnected with the hanging. And when asked how he accounted for the marks of tying on Shorthouse's wrists and ankles, and for the dislocated skeleton, he had replied somewhat curtly that he was unable to account for them and that moreover, being likewise unable to shake Furbelow's evidence, he could see no possible answer to the problem beyond *felo de se*. At this Fen's heart misgave him; it was by no means impossible, he reflected, that Mudge was right and that he himself was re-enacting the error of the preposterous Mr Blenkinsop. And so it was only because he had an innate detestation of abandoning anything in mid-career that he went ahead with his inquiries.

He found Peacock without difficulty, and they went to the residents' lounge to drink coffee. As opposed to the bar – which was darkly gothic, suggestive of oubliettes, halberds, *ceintures de chasteté* and other fearsome medieval contrivances – the room offered, despite its size, an approximation at least of bourgeois domesticity and comfort. There was even, about its solid, magazine-littered tables, its soft carpets and rugs, and its flowered chintz ottomans and armchairs, a suggestion of unintended parody, which was accentuated by the spasmodic apparition of incongruously dinner-jacketed waiters, bearing that variety of metal coffee- and tea-pot which seems designed specifically to burn the fingers. A perennial quiet invested it, emanating perhaps from the one or two old gentlemen who are always to be found in such places, nodding their lives out over newspapers, to the rattle of coffee-spoons and the periodic heavy vibration of buses passing outside the windows. Conversation, within its walls, became muted automatically to an undertone.

Peacock showed great willingness to be questioned. 'Naturally,' he said, 'I'll help you in any way I can, though I must confess to start with that I regard Shorthouse's death as an almost unmixed blessing . . .' His voice had a curiously hollow, rasping quality. 'Obviously *I* had no reason to be fond of him . . . You've probably heard about my unfortunate outburst at rehearsal the day before yesterday. Luckily I have an alibi for the time he was killed.'

'Let me congratulate you,' said Fen dryly. 'You seem to be the only person in the whole of Oxford who has.'

'It's fortunate,' said Peacock. 'Decidedly fortunate.' He paused to pay the waiter. 'Just as it happened I was in the hotel manager's sitting-room, chatting and drinking beer, right up to midnight. Either he or his wife was with me the whole time.'

Peacock enunciated all this with the naïve triumph and self-importance of a Hellenic scholar who has unearthed some remote mythological allusion from the works of Hesiod. But Fen was comparatively unimpressed. After all, it was by no means necessary for a gamekeeper to be present whenever a rabbit fell into a trap . . . This train of thought, however, suggested an entirely fresh set of possibilities which plainly could not be examined at the moment.

'That is very lucky,' he agreed. 'In point of fact, though, I'm rather more interested in yesterday afternoon than in the time of Shorthouse's death.'

'Yesterday afternoon? But why?'

They all ask that, thought Fen sadly: they all ask that, and in each and every case I'm obliged to make some evasive and unlikely reply which puts them instantly on guard . . . 'For a reason,' he said with an effort, 'which I'll explain in a moment.'

Peacock accepted this without apparent curiosity. 'What do you want to know?'

'Simply what you yourself were doing.'

This was easily elicited. After lunch Peacock had been interrogated by Mudge, retiring subsequently to his room in order to meditate over the score of *Die Meistersinger*. There he had remained until Mudge rang up at about three to say that the theatre would henceforth be available for its usual purposes. Immediately after this he had telephoned Karl Wolzogen, and instructed him to attempt to get people together for a snap rehearsal at five.

'And I must say I was surprised,' Peacock added, 'at what

he managed to achieve in the time. Fortunately I'd managed to warn a few people earlier on that there *might* be such a rehearsal . . . At about a quarter to five Karl appeared to report progress. Then we went straight to the theatre.'

'Together, of course.'

'As a matter of fact, no. Karl stayed behind—'

'In pursuance,' Fen quoted Wilkes, 'of some bodily necessity?'

'If you like to put it that way.' Peacock frowned, apparently in deprecation of this harmless euphemism. 'In any case, he wasn't long after me in getting to the theatre.'

Lurking in lavatories . . . The possibility, Fen remembered, had occurred to him before. And it was now evident that either Peacock or Karl Wolzogen could have slipped into Elizabeth's bedroom unobserved by Joan Davis as she approached it from the stairs. Unhappily there was a general absence of exactness over the chronology of this particular half-hour – and, still more unhappily, it remained impracticable to ascribe the attacks on Elizabeth with any certainty to either Peacock or Wolzogen, since some third person, in wait outside the bedroom, might conceivably have been disturbed by the opening of Peacock's door and have fled for shelter to a convenient bathroom, emerging to make his assault only when the coast was clear. The corridor was, of course, carpeted, and Joan Davis, approaching beyond its bend, would have been inaudible . . . These tortuous considerations, however, were leading nowhere. What they amounted to ultimately was that Elizabeth's attacker might have been absolutely anyone. Yet again Fen was seized with exasperation at the unique elusiveness of this case. Whenever one seemed to see, on the horizon, some definite, incontrovertible conclusion, it faded as one neared it and at last vanished like a mirage, leaving one confronted with yet a further vista of featureless desert . . .

'You're going to the inquest, of course?' Peacock was looking at his watch.

'Yes. But we're in good time.'

'I was only thinking that in view of the newspapers there might be rather a crowd.'

This was true enough. The death of Edwin Shorthouse, though in part eclipsed by the haphazard goings-on of the United Nations Organization, had at least reached the front pages. Fen finished his coffee.

'You haven't been subpoenaed, I suppose?'

'No, thank God,' said Peacock, 'though Stapleton has . . . We'd better go straightaway if we're to get in. I'll fetch my coat and join you in the foyer.'

As he waited: 'Something else will have to happen,' Fen thought. 'Something else will have to happen if I'm to get a grip on this business.' But that it would happen so soon and so horribly he had at this stage no reason for suspecting.

The sun was making a timorous debut as they walked down Cornmarket towards the town hall in St Aldate's, in a room of which the inquest was to be held. Peacock had been right about the crowd, and it was only thanks to the fact that Fen was known to the sergeant in charge that they got in at all. Virtually everyone was there: Adam, Elizabeth, Joan, Karl, Boris, Judith, Mudge, Furbelow, Dr Rashmole and, more surprisingly, the Master, smiling complacently beneath a neat black Homburg hat and attended by Beatrix Thorn. The room was bleak, with a dusty and uneven wooden floor, large, grimy windows, and a substantial supply of rickety, uncomfortable chairs, varied here and there by ancient school desks, black with inkstains and graven to the edge of collapse with the names of the generations of their former occupants. A platform at one end supported the coroner's chair, table, and inkpot. The representatives of the press were segregated like lepers to the right of this, yawning, fidgeting, sneezing, and staring about them. Opposite them was the table reserved for the jury. The atmosphere was sub-arctic. There was a subdued and persistent chattering.

'By the by,' said Fen, as he and Peacock pushed their way towards two vacant chairs immediately behind Adam, Elizabeth and Joan Davis, 'there's one question I forgot to ask: when you set off for the opera-house yesterday, did you see anyone you knew hanging about in your corridor?'

But this forlorn hope was instantly crushed, and Fen, exacerbated, left Peacock and sought out Mudge.

'We're after a verdict of suicide, all right,' said the Inspector in answer to his queries, 'and as regards the Nembutal, we're treating that, as you know, as a separate affair.'

'You're not going to attempt to *charge* anyone?'

'We haven't a case,' Mudge admitted 'unless something fresh turns up.'

'That stool that was found overturned in the dressing-room – has it been tested?'

'Yes. There are the marks of Shorthouse's shoes on it, his prints, and some very much older prints which obviously have nothing to do with it. Exactly what you'd expect in a case of suicide.'

'Exactly what you'd expect,' Fen grumbled, 'from an intelligent murderer.' He debated whether to take this opportunity of telling Mudge about the attacks on Elizabeth, decided against it, and went back to his seat. Elizabeth turned round in her seat to speak to him.

'Professor Fen,' she said, 'I owe you an apology.'

'What nonsense.'

Elizabeth was persistent. 'I was unbearably rude to you last night.'

'"Unnoticeably" is the epithet you want,' said Fen, smiling at her. 'Well, Adam, how are you feeling?'

'He has a hangover,' said Elizabeth reprovingly. Adam nodded his confirmation of this melancholy diagnosis. Joan Davis said:

'Well, quite candidly, I'm frightened.'

'I've already told you,' said Fen, 'that you've no need to worry.'

Presently the jury filed in. It consisted of five men and two women, in varying stages of bewilderment and self-consciousness. The representatives of the press stared at it and began savagely shaking their fountain-pens to make the ink flow. The foreman of the jury, a small, epicene creature with a piping voice and an arrogant manner, made little jokes about the uncomfortable chairs. This Fen observed with secret misgiving.

Shortly afterwards the coroner himself appeared, and amid a hasty stubbing-out of cigarettes the proceedings began.

Chapter Seventeen

Much evil has been imputed to coroners, and doubtless with justification in some instances. The present official proved, however, to be an able and intelligent person, plainly anxious to get the verdict in with the minimum of fuss and irrelevance. The jury was sworn, and expressed its unwillingness to view the body. The formalities of identification followed. Dr Rashmole was then called to give evidence as to the cause of death.

'Respiratory failure,' he announced, 'resulting from dislocation of the second and third cervical vertebrae.'

'You have no doubt about this?'

'None whatever. The post mortem signs were unmistakable.'

'Did your examination of the body lead you to any further conclusions?'

'Yes. The general condition of the deceased suggested to me that at some time previous to death he had taken a quantity of some barbiturate poison. In view of this I arranged for the gastro-intestinal contents to be analysed.'

'What would have been the effects of this poison?'

'Drowsiness, merging eventually into coma. Also, in all probability, a state of mental confusion, perhaps combined with loss of memory.'

'In your opinion, this poison could not have caused death?'

'It *could* have caused death, yes,' said Dr Rashmole testily. 'But in point of fact it didn't.'

He stood down, and was replaced by an analyst.

'You tested the contents of the deceased's stomach and intestines?'

'I did.'

'With what result?'

'I diagnosed the presence of some seventy grains of a barbiturate hypnotic.'

'Can you be more specific?'

'Unfortunately that is difficult. There's a great diversity of barbiturate products – I could name off-hand at least twenty-five – which differ only very slightly in their chemical formulae, and for which as a result it's virtually impossible to test. The only thing one can say with certainty is that it's some form of Barbitone or Veronal.'

Joan turned and whispered to Fen:

'That sounds a bit more hopeful.'

Fen grunted: 'You'll be all right,' he whispered back, 'provided it doesn't come out that you possess Nembutal . . . God bless that coroner, though. He does know what he's about. We shall probably get the whole thing finished with in time for a drink before lunch.'

A Miss Willis was called. She was young, foolish, and clothed with awe-inspiring elaboration.

'You are Dr Shand's maidservant?'

Miss Willis giggled and made some inaudible reply.

'You must speak up,' said the coroner, 'or the jury won't hear you . . . Did you answer the telephone in Dr Shand's house late on the evening of Monday last?'

Miss Willis giggled again, and after a pause for recovery was understood to assent.

'At what time was this?'

'Something like ten past eleven, sir.' On this occasion Miss Willis's reply fractionally anticipated her giggles. The coroner, evidently interpreting this as a favourable sign, went on energetically:

'Can you not be more precise?'

'Oh, no, sir.'

'What was the message you received?'

'Oh, sir, it was someone said Mr Shorthouse was at the opera-house poisoned or the like, and would Dr Shand go round at once.'

'Was the speaker a man or a woman?'

'I couldn't say, sir. It was all in a kind of whisper.'

'Can you remember the exact words that were used?'

'Oh, no, sir, not possibly I couldn't.'

'Was the form of the words such that Mr Shorthouse himself might have been the speaker?'

'I – I *think* it might have been 'im.'

'You can't be more definite than that?'

It appeared, in the upshot, that Miss Willis could not be more definite than that. Fen saw the point of the question, and admired the tactics which lay behind it. Obviously that telephone call had to be explained away somehow if the theory of suicide were to stand.

Miss Willis retired, scarlet but triumphant, and Dr Shand took her place. He was a tall, grey-haired, stooping man who made no attempt to conceal his dislike of the proceedings. Immediately on receiving the message, he said, he had got out his car and driven straight to the opera-house.

'I had difficulty at first in finding anyone,' he added, 'but

146

on proceeding towards the dressing-rooms I met the stage door keeper, who pointed out Shorthouse's door to me. I opened it and discovered Shorthouse hanging by the neck from a rope attached to a hook in the ceiling.'

'There was no other person in the dressing-room?'

'No one whatever. I went on, with Furbelow's assistance' – the tone of Dr Shand's voice suggested that this had been exiguous – 'to cut down the body, and discovered that although respiration had ceased, the heart was still beating faintly.'

'Is this a common phenomenon in such cases?'

'If not common, at all events well enough attested to give me no surprise. I injected Coramine to stimulate the heart, and applied artificial respiration. But the action of the heart, which was very weak, ceased almost immediately. Afterwards I got in touch with the police.'

'In your opinion, how long could the heart go on beating after respiration had stopped?'

'For two or three minutes at the most.'

'It is therefore your opinion that the actual dislocation of the cervical vertebrae must have occurred some two or three minutes before you arrived?'

'That is so.'

'At what time did you arrive?'

'It was just on half past eleven.'

Mudge took the stand. Some inner unease caused him to give his evidence in tones of faint surprise, as though in retrospect he was unable to account for all the things he had seen and done. He described the dressing-room and its surroundings with great minuteness.

'Is it your conviction,' the coroner asked, 'that the only possible form of access to this room was by the door?'

'It is.'

'Had the room any cupboard, closet, or other hiding-place where a person might have remained concealed?'

'Decidedly not.'

Mudge went on to speak of the gin bottle and the glass, and to read out the analyst's report on them. Afterwards he described the fingerprint investigations. Fen noted with wry amusement that there was no reference to the skeleton or to the marks of tying on Shorthouse's wrists and ankles. The former point, of course, could quite easily be explained away. But the latter . . . He roused himself from his reverie at the coroner's final question.

'In your opinion, to what conclusion do all these circumstances point?'

'To the fact that the deceased met his death by suicide.'

There was a general murmur, more perhaps of disappointment than of surprise. Furbelow was called. He kept doggedly to his original story.

'You are quite certain, then, that no one entered or left the dressing-room after ten minutes past eleven?'

Furbelow was quite certain. The coroner questioned him a little longer, less, Fen suspected, in order to shake his story than to emphasize it in the minds of the jury, and he was allowed to stand down.

The next witness was Stapleton.

'You visited the deceased in order to discuss some private matter with him?'

'Yes. An opera I'd written, and on which I wanted his opinion.'

'He himself arranged the time and place?'

'That's so.'

'Were you surprised at the lateness of the hour suggested?'

'I was at the time, but I've learned since that he usually spent the evening in pubs and then returned to the theatre to go on drinking there. So I suppose that would account for it.'

'When you arrived at the dressing-room he was alone?'

'Yes.'

'At what time was this?'

'Shortly before eleven. That was the time we'd agreed on.'

'How long did you stay with him?'

'Not more than ten minutes. It was obvious almost at once that he hadn't even looked at the opera. What's more, he was pretty well fuddled. He talked in a vague rambling way about opera in general, but I saw there was no point in staying, so I didn't stay.'

'Did he seem to you to be in a suicidal frame of mind?'

Stapleton hesitated. 'I'm not quite sure what a suicidal frame of mind is . . . Certainly he was depressed, and there were one or two bursts of self-pity. But I can't say I had any suspicion that he might commit suicide.'

'You saw nothing unusual about the room?'

'No.'

'No sign, for instance, of a length of rope?'

'No. But I suppose there might have been rope hidden away somewhere.'

'Did you notice if there was a hook embedded in the ceiling?'

'I didn't notice at all.'

'Thank you, Mr Stapleton. That will be all.'

To Fen's surprise, Stapleton was followed by Charles Shorthouse, who proved to be the coroner's last witness.

'Mr Shorthouse, do you consider it possible, from your own knowledge of him, that your brother committed suicide?'

'Well, now . . .' The Master considered deeply. 'He was, of course, mad. And then Oxford seems to have a curious effect on some people. For example, there was a man came to see me only yesterday, pretending to be the English representative of the Metropolitan opera-house . . . I saw through him, though,' the Master added, 'from the very first instant.'

'But what reason have you for suggesting that your brother was insane?'

'Well, for one thing he was a nymphomaniac. Nymphomaniac,' the Master explained, 'one who has a mania for nymphs.' He paused innocently on this fragment of exegesis.

'You mean that he was obsessed with the opposite sex.'

'Exactly.' The Master appeared pleased at such ready percipience. 'He pursued women. And that, I presume, is an activity to be included in the definition of madness.'

There was a mild outbreak of amusement. The coroner regarded his witness warily.

'Do you suppose that such an – ah – predilection is likely as a rule to lead to suicide?'

'Conceivably not,' the Master admitted after a moment's thought. 'But he was nonetheless unbalanced. The whole of our family is more or less unbalanced.'

'But can't you give some *instance* to show that your brother was unbalanced?'

'He refused to finance the production of my *Oresteia*.'

The coroner became confused. 'I thought that Aeschylus—' he began, and then, pulling himself together: 'Very well, Mr Shorthouse. That will do for the present.' He turned now to the jury.

'Members of the jury, you have heard the ev—'

But he was not allowed to finish the sentence. The foreman of the jury was on his feet and clamouring for attention.

'Mr Coroner,' he piped, 'is it in order for me to ask a question?'

'You mean—' the coroner was manifestly annoyed – 'that you wish to recall one of the witnesses?'

'No, sir. I wish to call a new witness.'

'That would be very irregular. Are you sure that what you have to ask is relevant to the matter in hand?'

'Oh, yes, it's relevant all right,' said the foreman, and there was an unpleasant gleam in his eye.

'Who is it you wish to call?'

'I see she's here,' said the foreman. 'It's Miss Joan Davis.'

In the fractional hush which followed Joan twisted round and said desperately to Fen:

'What's all this about?'

'I don't know,' said Fen, and he looked worried. 'But keep your nerve, and above all, tell the exact truth.'

In response to the coroner's summons, Joan walked slowly to the witness-stand, clutching her handbag in fingers which trembled a little. The public, which had become apathetic and restless, stiffened to attentiveness. The foreman of the jury leaned forward impressively. Evidently he was enjoying his little moment.

'Miss Davis,' he said. 'I believe you have in your possession a quantity of a drug named Nembutal?'

'That's true.'

'Are you aware that this drug is one of the barbiturate group?'

'Certainly I am.'

'It's true, isn't it, that a large quantity of this drug has disappeared from your possession during the last few days – more than could be accounted for by its normal use?'

'Yes, but anyone could have—'

'Thank you, Miss Davis. Will you cast your mind back to the evening on which Mr Shorthouse died? After dinner you were, I believe, with a small gathering of friends in the bar of the Randolph Hotel.'

'Yes.'

'Did you, or did you not, make a remark to the effect that you would like to poison Mr Shorthouse?'

'Yes, but it was only a casual—'

'That's all, Miss Davis.'

'But you can't accuse—'

'I have no more questions for you.'

Fen, observing the interest of the reporters, put one hand over his eyes and groaned audibly. Joan lost her temper.

'Listen to me!' she exclaimed. 'Listen to me, you self-important little ape—'

But the coroner, while obviously sharing her distaste, was obliged to put a stop to this. Joan returned in anger to her chair.

'And now, perhaps,' said the coroner sardonically, 'I may be permitted to sum up what we have heard. But before I do so I would like, in view of the questions which have just been asked, to remind you of the function of this court. It is an inquisition, *and not a trial*. Your duty, members of the jury, is to decide whether the deceased met his death by accident, suicide, or murder: should you decide on the last of these three possibilities, it is open to you to name some particular person as the culprit. But it is *not* your duty, or even your right, to comment on any other aspect of the affair whatever. If you decide, as you surely must, that the deceased met his death by hanging, then the poison which, as we have heard, was taken by the deceased previous to his death – *but which did not actually cause his death* – is important only in so far as it bears on the central problem. We are concerned not with the person, if any, who *attempted* to kill this man, but with the person – if any – who actually *did* kill him. And as the evidence has shown, no such person can possibly exist.

'The testimony of the Inspector, of Dr Shand, and of the stage door keeper leave us no doubt on this point. Dr Shand has said that the dislocation of the neck must have occurred at 11.25 or even later. The stage door keeper has told us that no one entered or left the room after 11.10. Dr Shand has further stated that no one except the deceased was in the room when he entered it, and the Inspector has certified that it contains no possible hiding-place. Therefore unless we postulate any murderer capable of escaping through a skylight scarcely large enough to admit a bird, we cannot postulate any murderer at all; for to the best of my knowledge no means of hanging a man by remote control has yet been devised.

'So we are left with accident or suicide. Into the reasons militating against accident I need hardly enter; they will be sufficiently clear to all of you. It is of course remotely conceivable that the deceased, having placed his head in a noose, allowed the stool on which he was standing to slip away from beneath his feet, and was thus inadvertently hanged, but there is no clear reason why he should have made such a foolish experiment.

'On the other hand there would seem to be some evidence to support the theory of suicide. The deceased's brother has stated, though without offering any very substantial proof of his assertion, that the deceased was mentally unbalanced. Moreover – and this is more important – a medical witness has testified that one of the effects of a large dose of barbiturate, before coma supervenes, is to produce a condition of mental aberration. It is at least possible, therefore, that the deceased hanged himself while made temporarily insane by the influence of this drug. And the "outbursts of self-pity" to which another witness has referred make this a colourable hypothesis. As regards the telephone call to Dr Shand we have no clue. But it was made about the time when Furbelow was conducting Mr Stapleton to the stage door, and it is therefore not beyond conjecture that it was made by the deceased himself, from the instrument at the end of the corridor in which his dressing-room is situated. Feeling the effects of the drug, he may have attempted to call medical aid, and have succumbed subsequently to the mental disorder which the drug induces before that aid could reach him.

'As to this, however, there is no certainty, and it rests with you, the jury, to decide between a verdict of accident and one of suicide. That is all I have to say to you. Do you wish to retire to consider your verdict?'

After a few moments surreptitious argument the jury announced that they did wish to retire. The court adjourned. A good many people went out into St Aldate's to smoke. Fen went to interview Mudge.

'I don't trust that jury,' said the Inspector gloomily. 'They look an obstinate, muddle-headed lot to me. And as for the foreman . . .' He paused to meditate some adequately indelicate form of abuse.

'Who informed him,' Fen asked, 'about Joan Davis and the Nembutal?'

'Anonymous letter, I fancy. Someone has a grudge against the woman.'

'Or alternatively the murderer wants to suggest that the Nembutal and the hanging are unconnected.'

'So they must be,' said Mudge. 'Anyway, I'll have words with that smart-alec after the verdict's been brought in.'

Fen gave him news of the attacks on Elizabeth.

'*Lord*,' said Mudge in despair. 'What's going to happen next? All right, sir, I'll look into it.'

'I wish you joy,' said Fen. 'In my experience it's an unrewarding job . . . By the way, I suppose you've questioned Karl Wolzogen?'

'Yes. It seems he was in bed at the time Shorthouse died. Almost everyone was in bed,' Mudge added peevishly. He seemed distressed at the sloth of his witnesses. Fen left him to seek out the persons who had been present at the emergency meeting in the Randolph. His questions resulted in the information that its proceedings had been sufficiently widely reported to offer no clue regarding the identity of the person who had communicated Joan's unfortunate remark to the foreman of the jury.

In about half an hour they heard that the jury were on the point of returning, and crowded back to the scene of operations. Scarcely anyone doubted that the verdict would be suicide, but there was some curiosity as to whether anything would be said about the provenance of the Nembutal in the gin. The members of the jury looked harassed and exceedingly ill at ease. A hush fell as the foreman got to his feet.

'You have arrived at your verdict?'

'Yes, Mr Coroner. We find that the deceased was murdered by some person or persons unknown.'

Sensation.

'And we further find that an attempt was made to murder the deceased by Miss Joan Davis.'

After a moment's initial stupefaction, there was a roar of

155

excited chatter. Joan was very pale. The representatives of the press began making hysterical haste for the door. The coroner rapped for silence.

'I confess,' he said, regarding the jury with open detestation, 'that the processes of reasoning by which you have arrived at your verdict wholly elude me. Your decision will, however, be communicated by the police to the Director of Public Prosecutions, who will decide what is to be done. And no doubt you yourselves, as public-spirited citizens, will inform those in charge of the case by what esoteric method this murder was carried out.

'There is one other thing I have to say. You have seen fit to add a rider to your verdict charging a specific person with attempted murder. I would like to emphasize that that rider has no validity whatever, that it is not equivalent to an indictment, that the police are perfectly at liberty to ignore it if they choose, and that I personally regard it as a flagrant instance of grotesque and wanton irresponsibility. I would further ask the representatives of the press to deal with it with that discretion for which they are justly famed . . . That is all. The court is adjourned.'

'"Discretion",' Fen muttered to himself as he joined the rush for the doors. 'There is true optimism. "Jury Accuses Prima Donna of Attempted Slaying" . . . Oh, my dear paws.'

Chapter Eighteen

In the afternoon he visited a member of the jury and found that their deliberations had consisted almost exclusively of a monologue by the foreman. It was evident that he had been possessed by a kind of undirected malignancy against which his dimmer-witted colleagues had no defence. It was further evident that the verdict of murder had depended much less on the evidence than on the sensational conjectures of the newspapers, though no member of the jury had regarded the evidence of a suicidal frame of mind as adequate. This, Fen reflected, was just; it had all along been one of the weakest links in the police theory.

He telephoned Mudge and learned that the foreman of the jury had indeed received an anonymous letter. He had, however, burned it after mastering its contents – and at this Mudge's language became lurid. Fen bought an evening paper on the way home, and saw that his fears had been well-founded.

There ensued several days of feverish coming and going. Reporters pestered everyone remotely connected with the opera, including Fen, who, however, eluded the worst effects of their attentions by issuing statements so scandalous and incredible that no one dared print them. Elizabeth was kept under rigid surveillance. Adam went so far as to borrow a revolver, but found that even apart from being heavy to carry about, it bulged too conspicuously in his pocket; so he put it in a drawer in his dressing-room and instantly forgot about it (he was not aware that someone passing outside at the time observed and took note of the existence of the weapon). The aconitine had been extracted from the tea, and Mudge bustled to and fro engaged in fruitless inquisition. Beatrix Thorn and the Master settled at the 'Mitre'. It transpired that they at least could not have attacked Elizabeth, since there were witnesses to prove that they had been at home during the whole of the day. On the Friday, Judith Haynes and Boris Stapleton were married at a London register-office, with Adam, Joan and Elizabeth in attendance. Stapleton's health continued to deteriorate. In the midst of it all the new academic term began, and Fen became preoccupied with lecture notes and collection papers. He still found time, however, to visit occasionally the *Meistersinger* rehearsals, and it was during one of these visits that he spoke to Karl Wolzogen.

The old man was relaxing momentarily from his labours, which were naturally becoming more exigent and various as the day of the performance drew nearer. He wore a pair of disreputable flannel trousers and a leather jacket, from the breast pocket of which drooped a large red silk handkerchief. His gnome-like face was brown, eager, heavily lined, with a greying stubble about the chin, and he was absorbed in the rehearsal even though at present he was taking no active part in it.

'That Peacock,' he said, 'is a true Wagnerian conductor. He has the – *wie ists genannt?* – the flexibility which the *Meister* craved for and which Richter never had. I have seen or worked with them all, you understand – Toscanini, Bülow,

Richter, Nikisch, Mottl, Barbirolli, Beecham . . . All of them. I know the real thing when I see it, *glauben Sie mir*. This Peacock is good.'

Fen regarded him with interest. 'You're a very fanatical Wagnerian,' he said.

'*Aber natürlich*.' Karl always relapsed a little into his native language when he was talking to someone who could understand it. 'My whole life has been opera – and Wagner in particular, *selbstverständlich*. If my father had afforded to give me the musical education I should myself have been a conductor. But I began to learn too late. So I have always been régisseur, or producer, or call-boy. At the Weimar opera, when I was sixteen, I was call-boy . . . After that I was in many of the German opera-houses, and for a time in America. When the Nazis came I was too old for their ideas, and I hated that such fools should worship the *Meister*. I had preferred that they banned his performances. So I worked here, and then there was the war, and fools said: "Because Hitler is fond of Wagner we will not have Wagner in England". Hitler was also fond of your Edgar Wallace, with his stories of violence, but no one said that they were not to be read . . . Now it is better, and soon I shall return to my own country. But there is no Wagner there, and before I die I must hear the seven great operas once again. So at present I stay in England.' For a long time he meditated, then he said, in a slightly altered tone of voice: 'You, sir, you are investigating the death of this man?'

Fen shrugged. 'I was.'

'*Wäre es nicht besser—*'

'That the murderer should remain undiscovered? On the face of it, yes. But none of us has the right to assess the value of a human existence. All must be held valuable, or

159

none. The death of Christ and the death of Socrates,' Fen added dryly, 'suggest that our judgements are scarcely infallible . . . And the evil of Nazism lay precisely in this, that a group of men began to differentiate between the value of their fellow-beings, and to act on their conclusions. It isn't a habit which I, for one, would like to encourage.'

Karl was silent for some moments before replying.

'*Veilleicht haben Sie recht*,' he said at last. 'But I am glad he is dead.' His voice sank to a whisper. 'I am glad this man is dead.'

The dress-rehearsal of act one was on the Saturday; of acts two and three on the Sunday. Marvels of artistry and effort had been performed in the meantime, and any anxiety which may have been aroused by the belated substitution of a new Sachs was now dispelled. Fen attended the rehearsal of act two with Elizabeth. When it was over, at half past six in the evening, Adam joined them.

'We progress,' he said cheerfully. 'It should be all right tomorrow.'

'You'll get a good house,' said Fen amiably, 'if only because of poor Joan's notoriety.'

'We're booked out for the whole run,' Adam told him. 'Sensation-seekers are hardly the kind of audience we want, but no doubt their money will please Levi as much as anybody else's.'

'How is Joan taking it?' Fen asked. 'I haven't spoken to her for a day or two.'

'Stoically enough, I think. It hasn't been so bad recently . . . I suppose the police aren't going to charge her?'

'They haven't enough evidence – though I believe they still regard the dope and the hanging as unconnected.'

'Aren't they unconnected?'

'I think not – the anonymous letter to the foreman of the jury suggests as much – but I've no means of proving it, unfortunately. It may be, of course, that that anonymous letter was prompted by simple malice, but I've not yet succeeded in discovering anyone who dislikes Joan . . . By the way, what happens next?'

'Scene one of the last act,' said Adam. 'Since we're behind schedule, we're leaving scene two till tomorrow morning. The chorus has been told it can go home.'

'I wonder,' said Fen pensively, 'if a drink—'

'I'll tell you what.' Elizabeth was groping in her bag for a notebook and pencil. 'We can take this opportunity of getting my interview done. All right?'

'Decidedly all right,' said Fen, pleased. He reflected briefly. 'The era of my greatest successes,' he began, 'may be said, roughly speaking, to extend from the time when I first became interested in detection to the present moment, which sees me engaged on a case as baffling and complex as any I ever—'

But here, to his annoyance, he was interrupted by Judith Haynes, who came rapidly up the gangway and said:

'You haven't seen Boris anywhere, have you?'

Evidently the girl was worried. They could hardly make out her expression in the semi-darkness, but her voice was urgent, and the hand which she laid on the back of one of the seats trembled perceptibly.

'I haven't,' said Elizabeth. 'That's to say, not for the last half-hour. I thought he was with you.'

'He was until a few minutes ago. But now I can't find him anywhere.'

'Perhaps he's gone home.'

'He wouldn't have done that,' said Judith. Floodlights were

turned on and threw a halo about her fair hair. 'At least, not without telling me.'

'But surely' – Elizabeth spoke gently – 'there's nothing to worry about?'

'He wasn't feeling at all well. It's been getting worse all afternoon . . . Please help me.'

She was so near to tears that there was no possibility of rejecting the appeal. Fen and Adam separated to search the theatre. Ten minutes later, they met at the foot of the iron ladder which led from the top corridor of dressing-rooms through a trap-door on to the flat roof. Adam by now was wearing a great-coat over the green doublet and hose in which he had been impersonating a sixteenth-century knight of Franconia.

'Who are you?' said Fen. 'I don't know you from Adam.' He laughed very merrily at this; Adam did not join him.

'There's no sign,' he reported instead. 'I think the man must have left. Obviously that's what he'd do if he were feeling ill.'

'Yes, possibly.' Fen was grave again. 'But at the same time, I agree with the girl that he'd almost certainly have told her if he intended to do that.'

'Well, you don't think he's been kidnapped, do you?'

'I wouldn't know at all . . . It's simply that I don't like the sound of this "illness", particularly as there seems to be someone running around with a whole pharmacopoeia of poisons in his pocket . . . Come and help me look on the roof.'

'Have you got a torch? It must be quite dark now, and one doesn't want to topple over the edge.'

Fen felt in the pocket of his raincoat, and after bringing to light successively a grubby handkerchief, a half-empty packet of cigarettes, a copy of the *Imitation of Christ*, and a small woolly bear named Thomas Shadwell, found his torch.

Outside it was bitterly cold; Adam shivered and turned up the collar of his coat. No stars were visible, and the moon had not yet risen, but beneath a street lamp they could see the front of the Playhouse in Beaumont Street, and farther to the left the light from the foyer of the Randolph Hotel winked rapidly and was again still as someone pushed in through the revolving doors. The footsteps of a single wayfarer passing along St John Street were preternaturally clear and sharp. Adam, who disliked heights, felt a mild but decided nausea; the discovery which they shortly made, however, was sufficient to drive other considerations from his mind.

Boris Stapleton lay prone, about half-way between the skylight which penetrated the ceiling of Edwin Shorthouse's dressing-room and the little hut (its door now creaking lugubriously in the wind) which housed the machinery of the lift. Adam hardly needed to be told that he was dead, though there were no marks of violence on the body, except for the bruises occasioned by its fall. Traces of vomit were nearby. The good-looking young face, when they turned it over, betrayed nothing but a faint astonishment.

Chapter Nineteen

As well as possible, they lowered Stapleton's body down the ladder and carried it to Shorthouse's dressing-room, which had remained unoccupied since his death. It was a peculiarly exhausting task, which left them panting and unsteady. Fortunately they met no one.

'Well,' Adam gulped as he straightened himself, 'what do we do now?'

'Telephone Mudge, will you, and tell him what's happened.' Fen was smoothing back his unruly hair. 'But don't breathe a word to anyone else – particularly Judith.'

'Surely she ought to be—'

'I'm afraid,' said Fen grimly, 'that when she gets the news she'll break down. And there are some things I must ask her before that happens.'

'How did he die?'

'Arsenic, I fancy.'

Adam went to the telephone. Downstairs, the orchestra was tuning up for the third act; the oboe A droned out, encircled by bare fifths; the flutes were indulging in bravura displays; the tuba honked despondently. Fen bent down again to examine Stapleton's body. Despite the temperature of the roof, there was still a little warmth in it; but the man was thin, wasted, almost skeletal. The skin disease on his cheeks, throat, and chin resembled eczema. There was a strange, very faint odour resembling that of garlic. Repressing a slight shudder of disgust, Fen opened the mouth and felt for the tongue; it was much furred. The eyelids were red and puffy. Fen examined the finger-nails, noticed that there was a white band running across them, and turned his attention to the hair, and afterwards to the palms of the hands, which were hard and horny. Then he went to the wash-basin, and was soaping himself industriously when Adam returned.

'Mudge,' said Adam gloomily, 'was very much upset. I suppose he's beginning to realize that what with this and the attack on Elizabeth his suicide theory's suffering a lot of shocks . . . Anyway, he's coming here immediately. Have you discovered anything?'

Fen was drying his hands with a handkerchief; there appeared to be no towel in the room. 'I was right about the arsenic. And it's chronic – it must have been going on for some weeks.'

Adam kept his eyes averted from the face of the corpse; Fen had left the mouth open, and it gaped disagreeably. 'No wonder,' said Adam with an effort, 'that he was ill. I suppose if he'd only had the sense to see a doctor—'

'Exactly. He needn't have died.' Fen, about to return the damp handkerchief to his pocket, thought better of it, and put it instead on the dressing-table. 'That skin disease is a normal symptom of arsenical poisoning. But the fact that he'd suffered from eczema on some previous occasion made him unsuspicious.'

They both lit cigarettes. 'What makes it so unpleasant,' said Adam bitterly, 'is that whoever was poisoning him must have been aware that he'd rather die than stay out of the production, and have traded on it . . . And now Judith is a widow, after two days of marriage, and – oh, it's damnable.' After a pause he went on: 'And I can't see the motive for it, unless he knew something about Edwin's death . . . Could it be suicide?'

'Unheard-of,' said Fen without hesitation. 'If he'd wanted to commit suicide he'd have given himself one good dose, not a series. And anyway, why *should* he commit suicide? He'd just got married. To all appearance he was exceedingly happy.'

Adam nodded sombrely. 'How can arsenic be got?' he inquired. 'That is, without openly buying it?'

'In all sorts of ways. It can be extracted from fly-papers, and weed killers and rat poisons, and sheep dip and God knows what else . . . However,' Fen added, 'I'd better go and see Judith. It looks at present as if she'll be our sole witness. Will you wait here until I get back? Repel all boarders – except, of course, the police.'

On his way down the stairs he came upon Furbelow, and was reminded by the encounter of a problem which for some days he had been intending to clear up.

'Furbelow,' he said, 'did you have instructions from Mr Shorthouse not to disturb him when he was in his dressing-room?'

The question evidently stirred latent fires of resentment. Furbelow even forgot himself so far as to spit, though in rather a dry-mouthed ineffectual fashion.

'Ah, that he did,' he burst out. 'Some o' these theatre folk, they fancy they're God Almighty 'Isself. The first night 'e was 'ere I went into 'is dressing-room quite 'armless-like, to look if I might 'ave dropped something, an' what does 'is 'ighness do but tell me 'e'll wring my neck if I ever as much as put me nose inside again. Called me a thief, 'e did.' Ecstatic with rage, Furbelow hissed at Fen, like a goose. 'I wouldn't 'a' gorn in there again, not if the devil 'ad bin after me with 'is flesh-'ooks.'

Being unable to conceive any reliable method of putting a stop to this homiletics, Fen pursued his way, leaving Furbelow yelping indignantly behind him. It was unlikely, he thought, that the personnel of the opera were unaware of this incident; Furbelow was not the man to return contumely with silence. And that suggested that Edwin Shorthouse had been responsible for at least one circumstance which might have facilitated his own death.

Fen made his way into the wings. The third act had begun. Sachs sat engrossed in his folio; David was creeping into the room with the air of a particularly small mouse braving the slumbers of a particularly large cat. The wood-wind chattered vivaciously, but without confidence. Laying his basket on a table, David began to examine its contents, with one eye fixed apprehensively on his master. But after a time he became wholly preoccupied with cakes, ribbons, and sausages, and the sound of Sachs turning a page of the folio, underlined as it was by a downward rush of strings, threw him into something approaching a panic.

'Yes, Master!' he quavered. 'Here!'

Rich and sombre, the cellos enunciated the *Wahn* theme, that brilliantly contrived vein of melancholy which relieves and balances the whole great comedy . . . And on the opposite side of the stage Fen saw Judith talking to Rutherston. In another moment she had caught his eye and had slipped round the back to join him.

'Have you found him?' she said eagerly.

Fen spoke to her with great gentleness. 'No, I'm afraid not. Will you answer one or two questions?'

'Y-yes, but—'

'I wouldn't bother you if it wasn't important. How long have you and your husband been in Oxford?'

'Oh . . . about three weeks. But please—'

'And your husband hasn't been well during that time?'

'No . . . It's – it's been chiefly that horrible skin disease. And he *won't* see a doctor . . .'

'Can you give me more details of his illness?'

'But why? Why? I don't see—'

'As a matter of fact,' said Fen, 'I know something about diseases, and I fancy I have an idea what's wrong with him. If you can tell me the symptoms, I'll put them before a doctor, and we can at least get some suitable medicine made up.' Fen spoke with an effort. He was at the best of times averse to lying, except for the sake of amusement, and he was vividly conscious of the cruelty of what he was doing. But there seemed no other way. 'Presumably,' he added, 'your husband would have no objection simply to taking medicine – particularly if it came from you.'

The girl nodded. 'It's – it's very kind,' she stammered. 'I'll tell you all I can . . . He's got a kind of laryngitis as well as the skin disease. And he's been sick a lot, and he's had diarrhoea, and he's hardly been eating at all. Oh, and he complained that his muscles were hurting and that his hands sometimes went numb . . . I – I think that's all.' She attempted a smile. 'And quite enough, too.'

'There are two possibilities,' Fen went on ruthlessly (afterwards he was to look back on this little episode as from his point of view the most sheerly objectionable in the whole case). 'There are two possibilities, and one of them is food poisoning.'

'Poisoning?' There was alarm in Judith's voice.

'Ptomaine. You know. It isn't necessarily dangerous . . . Have you been having your meals at the place where you're staying?'

'Yes. I've cooked them for him. The landlady lets me use the kitchen.' Judith's eyes grew wider. 'But surely *I* can't have been responsible . . . Besides, I've been eating the same things as he had, and I'm all right.'

'Exactly. It mayn't be the food. It mayn't even be poisoning at all . . . But has he been drinking much?'

'No, hardly at all. Only once before that morning in the "Bird and Baby".'

'Then don't worry,' said Fen. Now that he had heard everything of importance he was anxious to finish with the interview.

'But where is he now?' the girl asked.

'As Elizabeth suggested, he's probably gone home. It's not impossible, is it, that he missed you, and imagined *you* were ahead of *him*? Maybe he was misinformed by someone . . . I think your best plan is to go to Clarendon Street and see if he's there. He doesn't appear to be in the theatre, but if he turns up I'll tell him where you are.'

Fen left her and returned to Shorthouse's dressing-room. 'Disgusting,' he murmured to himself. 'Disgusting but unfortunately unavoidable.' Adam, whose vigil had already provoked a faint unease, was pleased at his return.

'I was wondering,' Adam said, 'just what Stapleton was doing on the roof.'

Fen sat down; he was tired and dispirited. 'Trying to get air,' he said briefly. 'He must have felt an attack of asphyxia coming, and gone outside in the hope of relieving it. The roof has no importance in itself.'

In a few moments more Mudge arrived with a police doctor. Luckily the latter was not Dr Rashmole, whose necrophilious exuberance Fen felt would have been unendurable in the present circumstances. He examined the body, and provisionally confirmed Fen's diagnosis. Fen gave Mudge a digest of the information he had received from Judith; its effect did not appear to be enlivening.

'Well, sir,' said Mudge blankly, 'there seems to be only one answer to *this* problem.'

'Impossible,' Fen replied waspishly. 'The girl was utterly devoted to him. She'd no more have killed him than I would.'

'There are people who can act, sir,' said Mudge platitudinously. 'And it wouldn't be the first time a love-affair's gone sour and ended in murder.'

'Would she have admitted to preparing his meals if she'd been poisoning him?'

'Of course she would.' Mudge, too, was becoming a trifle annoyed. 'The landlady knew all about it, and it would have been insane to deny the fact.'

'Perhaps,' Adam suggested with singular lack of penetration, 'some third person put the poison in the sugar, or in some other ingredient.'

He looked at them hopefully, but neither Fen nor the Inspector made any effort to point out that if this were the truth Judith too would probably be dead. The two men were, in fact, becoming unnecessarily heated. In Fen this was probably due to a reaction from his conversation with Judith; in the Inspector, to a growing belief that Fen was wilfully and unnecessarily complicating every aspect of the case he could lay hands on.

'It's by no means impossible, you know,' said Fen, 'that

Stapleton was regularly getting something to eat or drink from an outsider.'

'Not impossible, no,' said Mudge obstinately. 'But wouldn't his wife have known about it, if they were as intimate as you maintain?'

'I don't care,' Fen snapped. 'I decline absolutely to believe that she had anything to do with it. Haven't you got eyes in your head? Can't you see the child was in love with him?'

'And can't *you* see,' said the Inspector, 'that what you're trying to do is to fabricate another impossible murder?'

They stared at one another with open antagonism. And it was at that moment that the door opened and Judith herself entered the room.

'Professor Fen,' she said, 'I heard you'd come up here, and I wondered if—'

Then she saw the body which lay huddled on the floor.

The words died on her lips. She stood absolutely still. Her cheeks still glowed from the exertion of running up the stairs, but there was an area of dead whiteness about her nose and mouth. She made no attempt to approach the body. After a moment she began to sob – a slow, mechanical dry-eyed, almost soundless sobbing. For a time the four men stood helpless. Then the doctor tried to touch her, and she pushed him away with the gesture of a petulant child. The sobbing grew slower and at last ceased.

'You won't cut him up,' she whispered. And then her voice rose suddenly to a scream, a horrifying, ridiculous wail like that of a terrified cat: '*God help you if you touch him! God help you!*'

Adam took off his overcoat and laid it over the gaping, witless face. He was aware that the distant music had stopped

– aware, too, that it had stopped because he was not there to make his entry. He heard the call-boy chanting his name on the floor below, but he made no move.

After the rehearsal Fen walked back towards the 'Mace and Sceptre' with Adam, Joan and Elizabeth. Joan broke the long silence by saying:

'I wonder if they took my advice – to avoid having children at first . . . If they didn't, it may be a consolation to Judith to—'

It was Fen's turn to lose his temper. 'A consolation,' he repeated savagely. 'Yes, perhaps it may. But you still seem to forget that murder's been done, and that someone will sooner or later hang for it.'

'You don't think that Judith—'

'She didn't kill her husband. Of course not. But there was the murder of Shorthouse as well. Let's keep our chatter about "consolation" for the time when everything's cleared up.'

Elizabeth said gently: 'You haven't a clue, Professor Fen?'

'None,' said Fen more soberly. 'Not the vestige of an idea . . . You'd better cut me out of your series, Elizabeth.'

They went on in silence to the hotel. Before they parted Fen said to Joan:

'I'm sorry I was so detestably rude.'

She looked steadily at him. '"Unnoticeably",' she said, and smiled. 'We're all on edge, and I agree that sentimental chatter isn't any help . . . You'll be at the performance tomorrow?'

'Of course. Good luck, if I don't see you before then.'

'Come backstage afterwards.'

'I'd like to . . . Again, my apologies.'

'Forgiveness isn't in order,' said Joan. 'So I'll risk quoting

Shakespeare to a Professor of English Literature . . . *"Let us not burden our remembrance with a heaviness that's gone"*.' She smiled again, and went with Adam and Elizabeth into the hotel.

Chapter Twenty

Before the culmination of the case there was respite of a little less than twenty-four hours. The second scene of act three was rehearsed on the Monday morning, a week after Shorthouse's death. Substitutes were quickly found for Judith, who had withdrawn from the production and yet refused to go back to her parents, and for Stapleton. Rutherston gave a final impassioned address in which he begged the chorus to try and look like sixteenth-century Nurembergers instead of like an elementary eurhythmics class. The autopsy on Stapleton, which it had been impossible to waive, was not expected to produce definite results until the Tuesday morning. There was to be no work on the Monday afternoon until the curtain went up at six-thirty on the first performance.

Adam and Elizabeth spent the afternoon at the hotel. The events of the last few days had somehow contrived to cast a shadow over their relationship. A self-consciousness, almost a coldness, had grown up between them, the more difficult to dispel as the reasons for it were either too obscure or, it seemed, too inadequate to be dealt with directly. Neither was happy; their old careless intimacy had gone. In both, the faculty of criticism had been sharpened to include trivial and even imaginary offences. Elizabeth felt that Adam was becoming too tyrannical and overbearing, and began to regret (though with a sense of treachery) the days of her independence. Adam felt that Elizabeth was becoming touchy, irascible, and over-sensitive. Both saw in this development the notorious disillusionment which is said to follow the first romantic months of marriage, both half-resigned themselves to it, and both, as a consequence, confirmed and strengthened it.

Its causes were various. The impact of violent death had left them nervous, though they scarcely recognized the fact. Mere physical apprehension was only a part of it; there was also a suppressed atavism, a superstitious horror, still potent from the remote origins of the race, of the inexplicable. It was unconscious, but it was there. In Adam's case it was complicated partly by the strain of the final rehearsals (the death of Shorthouse having resulted in an abnormally high pressure of work for everyone) and partly by a temporary, irrational reaction against the disorderliness which has characterized the theatrical profession at all times and everywhere; in Elizabeth's by the constant surveillance on which Adam insisted. She was one of those who have an urgent, innate need of occasional solitude – and the war has shown, if proof be needed, that such people, when forced to be continually gregarious, become fretful and in extreme cases even insane.

They did not speak of these matters, being indeed only half conscious of them. Nor was their criticism of each other explicit; at most it was a matter of hints. But they were aware of the estrangement, and, by seeking for explanations of it more or less complimentary to themselves, accentuated it. The progess of their *malaise* had not of course reached as yet a point which could be described as crucial; it was reversible as and when they chose. Unluckily, neither of them was inclined to make the first move.

During the afternoon Adam slept, and was troubled with nightmares. When he awoke, dry-mouthed and with a feeling of nausea, there was only one of them that he could remember. He had seemed to be driving along a country road, and had come in sight of a large, grey, low-built, part-medieval building. Though he had never seen it before, he knew instinctively that its name was Oldacre Priory. He entered one of its rooms, which was sparsely furnished and hung with tattered banners. The place seemed to be a museum. There was no life in it, but he was later to find that there were creatures which moved. He opened a door which gave on to a courtyard. For a moment it seemed quiet, and then the building began to vibrate with a heavy tramping, and a file of armoured knights came into view. He was aware that there were no men inside the armour, either alive or dead. Nor were the things robots. They were mere accumulations of matter, moved purposively by some force outside themselves. They did not see him, but there was something about them which made him withdraw, very quickly and quietly, into the room of the banners, close the door, and lean for a moment against it to catch his breath. Then he started to run.

He ran quietly and rapidly through room after room of that vast, deserted place, seeking a way out. There was no sound save for the distant trampling of the knights. By this, in so far as his confusion and panic allowed, he regulated his course, keeping as far away from it as possible. At last, after what seemed an eternity, he came out at the end of an immensely long gallery. There was a figure standing motionless at the farther end, and until it moved he took it for a waxwork or a statue. Then, quite suddenly, he saw that it was Elizabeth, and that her jaws were tied together with a band of rotting linen, as are the jaws of a person long dead. She began moving swiftly towards him, and he – not in love, not in welcome, but in unendurable fear – ran towards her. As she came nearer, he saw that the linen band had given way, and that the lower jaw was hanging loose. He reflected, insanely, that this would not hamper a person who no longer spoke or ate or breathed. In the middle of the gallery they met in a clutching embrace, and it seemed to him that his heart burst with the horror of it.

He awoke trembling, and for some moments struggled dazedly to assimilate the somnolent, matter-of-fact atmosphere of the hotel lounge. Near him, Elizabeth sat at a table writing letters. When his jangled nerves were a little quietened, he went over to her.

'I've just had' – he spoke hesitantly – 'rather a horrible dream.'

'Have you, dear?' She was brisk and indifferent. 'I'm sorry . . . But for God's sake don't tell me about it. There are few things duller than someone else's dream.'

The realities came rushing back. This was a worse nightmare than the other had been. 'Elizabeth,' he burst out, 'what's the matter with us?'

'My dear, I couldn't say. I wasn't aware that there was anything the matter with *me* . . . Do you mind if I finish this letter?'

'Yes I do mind. I want to talk seriously to you.'

'Must it be in public?' Elizabeth murmured.

'There's no one listening . . . Darling, our marriage has gone wrong somewhere.'

'This sounds,' said Elizabeth judicially, 'like the beginning of a scene in a ninth-rate British film.'

'Please listen to me. I know one talks clichés on these occasions, but I'll do my best not to be trite . . . I want to know if there's anything *I* can do to help us to get back.'

'To get back?' Elizabeth spoke with polite incomprehension.

'To what we felt, for example, on our honeymoon.'

Elizabeth looked up at him, and her eyes were unsympathetic. 'Is that so very desirable? We'll have to get our marriage on a rational basis sooner or later. It can't be expected that we shall go on slobbering over one another all our lives.'

'I'm sorry,' said Adam bitterly, 'if my poor attempts to make you happy are to be classified as "slobbering".'

'Don't give way to self-pity, my dear. It's never a very agreeable sight.'

Adam controlled himself with an effort. 'I apologize,' he said. 'I've no doubt that there are many things I do which irritate you. But I wish you'd tell me about them, and then perhaps I can remedy the matter.'

'My dear,' said Elizabeth, and it was this reiterated, meaningless form of address which exacerbated Adam as much as anything else – 'my dear, if you haven't the sense to see your own defects, no catalogue from me will do any good. One doesn't make a blind man see by reeling off a list of flowers.'

'It doesn't occur to you that you yourself may not be entirely perfect?'

Elizabeth's anger rose to the surface. 'Obviously I'm not perfect. But that doesn't alter the fact that you're being damnably uncivil.'

'I was simply trying to get to the bottom of this – this trouble between us.'

'You go about it in a peculiar way.' Elizabeth rose, collecting her letters and notepaper. 'Obviously you won't let me finish what I'm doing. I'm going upstairs. Will you leave me undisturbed, please?'

She walked out of the lounge. Adam returned miserably to his chair. This was far worse than their first quarrel; this was cold and vehement. Half unwillingly, they had come to a crisis.

It needed the events of that evening to dispose of it.

Joan Davis and George Peacock walked in the gardens of St John's College.

A dilute, pale-yellow sun was struggling to appear, but the air was damp and cold, so they walked quickly, Peacock with a long, sprawling stride, Joan with an occasional little running step in order to keep up with him. She reflected wryly that it was a long time since she had last inconvenienced herself, even to this small extent, for the sake of a man's company. Several times they encircled the great central lawn; Peacock did not seem anxious to make any change in their orbit.

'One feels,' Joan ventured, 'rather like a rat on a wheel. Or like those Alpine travellers who struggle through blizzards and always come back to the place they started from.'

He looked at her quickly. 'You're bored?'

'Of course not. I shouldn't stay if I were.'

For a time they walked on in silence. Peacock was not normally loquacious, and at present he seemed preoccupied to the point of rudeness. 'But of course it's my own fault,' Joan thought. 'It was I who suggested this walk, and the poor devil hadn't really much chance to refuse . . . No, that's absurd. He could very well have said he wanted to rest before the show. Presumably, then, he doesn't mind being with me all that much.'

Aloud she said: 'You're not nervous about tonight?'

He laughed. 'Horribly. The box-office tells me that Ernest Newman's going to be there.'

'What could be better?'

'A good many things could be better. Conducting Wagner in front of Ernest Newman must be rather like lecturing one of the cherubims on the nature of Deity . . . However, I shall probably survive.'

'You're satisfied with the way things have gone?'

'The way the cast has behaved,' he said, 'makes me feel very humble. Every one of you knows ten times as much about opera as I do, and yet you've worked like demons to produce the effects *I* wanted. I couldn't have been luckier.'

Joan was oddly moved. 'Don't be so absurd,' she answered warmly. 'We should have fought you tooth and nail if you hadn't so obviously known your job. And anyway it was to our own advantage. We shall probably get the credit for your ideas . . . What are you going to do when this run's over?'

'It depends on Levi . . . I think I may get a permament engagement here if *Meistersinger* comes off satisfactorily.'

'Then don't worry. The job's as good as yours.'

They paused, rather abstractly, to examine a robin which was hopping erratically about on the edge of the lawn. After a while Peacock said:

'May I ask a very personal question?'

'Of course.'

'You're not married, are you?'

'Not now. A few years ago I was, but I divorced my

husband. Our conjugal bliss lasted, I think, about thirteen hours from the time we left the church . . . However, that doesn't matter. It's finished, thank God.'

'Would you – you wouldn't consider marrying me, I suppose?'

Joan looked up at him. Her puckish face was twisted into a half-smile which oddly suggested the imminence of tears. 'Thank you,' she said. 'But would it be wise?'

'I know I'm not—'

'I mean from your point of view. Oughtn't you to marry someone much younger than I? "*My child*",' she quoted, '"*of Tristan and Isolde a grievous tale I know. Hans Sachs was wise and would not endure King Marke's woe*" . . . Not quite apposite, perhaps. You should think rather of Hofmannsthal's Marschallin . . .' And to herself she said: 'Why this inane, allusive chatter? Surely I'm old enough by now not to have my head turned by a proposal?'

Peacock spoke awkwardly. 'If you mean that you don't want—'

'I mean,' she interrupted him, 'that it's only fair to you to put the situation brutally. I'm thirty-five – by no means in the *fleur de mes jours*. I know,' she went on rapidly as he opened his mouth to speak, 'that mine is the age politely referred to as a woman's maturity. But the unfortunate thing about maturity is that it isn't youth, and a man who marries a mature woman is like a man doomed to make all his purchases in the second-hand shops.' She hesitated. 'You see what I mean?'

He bowed his head. 'I'm sorry,' he said. 'It was too presumptuous of me.' And abruptly he left her and went stalking across the lawn towards the garden front of the college.

As she watched him go, tears came to her eyes. That, she told herself bitterly, was what came of being sane and level-headed on the subject of marriage. Obviously he had thought she was only trying to avoid wounding him by a direct refusal. And every moment that passed was making it more and more impossible to re-open the subject. Her pride, she knew, would forbid her to go to him, hours later, and say: 'About our conversation this afternoon . . .' No, unthinkable. And yet he was too sensitive to make the offer a second time. Happiness was slipping away from her with his receding figure. Quickly, decide.

She ran after him. 'Wait for me!' she gasped. 'Wait for me!'

He stopped, turned. As she came nearer he saw that her eyes were sparkling, her cheeks red with the cold air. She came up with him, and hesitated, partly out of embarrassment, partly to catch her breath. He took her hand to his, and kissed her very quickly and gently on the lips.

'One gets the best things nowadays,' he said gravely, 'in the second-hand shops.'

Chapter Twenty-One

Beatrix Thorn and the Master sat in the lounge of the 'Mitre' hotel.

'Surely, Master, it will do you harm to drink so much beer.'

'I shall drink as much beer as I wish, Beatrix.'

'Of course. But you mustn't undermine your constitution.'

'My constitution was undermined years ago.'

'In that case we must take care that it doesn't collapse altogether.'

'When I collapse, I shall collapse, and that will be an end to it.'

'But you have a duty to posterity.'

'Posterity has never done anything for me . . . I wonder why Wilkes made such a curious request?'

'It strikes me as sinister.'

'No doubt he had his reasons. I'm thinking, Beatrix, of buying a small sports car.'

'Better not. You would find the noise unendurable.'

'But I *like* noise. You don't seem to realize that I *like* noise.'

'Nonsense, Master.'

'It *isn't* nonsense. If I want a small sports car, I shall have it.'

'Of course if you insist . . . But let me explain the disadvantages.'

'No, no.'

'In the first place—'

'I asked you to be quiet, Beatrix. I'm trying to think out the opening scene of my new opera.'

'I only wanted to say that—'

'Be quiet. How can I concentrate when you insist on talking about cars?'

'Very well, Master.'

'What was that?'

'I said, very well.'

'Oh.'

Karl Wolzogen climbed on to a bus at Carfax which took him to Headington. From there he walked towards Wheatley – a small, thin, stooping figure, trudging along with his hands thrust for warmth into the pockets of a disreputable overcoat. He had had that overcoat for so long that he had completely forgotten when and where it had been bought. Somewhere in Germany or Austria, certainly. He paused to examine the grease-stained tab sewn inside one of the cuffs. Friedrich Jensen, Wettinerstrasse 83D, Dresden. He remembered now – remembered, too, that there had been a girl who lived in the Wettinerstrasse, a dark girl, perhaps a *nachgedunkelte Schrumpfgermane*, or perhaps with Jewish blood. In the latter case, what would have happened to her? She had had no use for opera. '*Das alles ist altmodisch*,' she had said. But he was old-fashioned too. As he grew older he lived more and more in the past. It meant that the end was not far off, and he was sufficiently satiated with living to be indifferent. Except perhaps for the loneliness which had come as a reward for his exclusive devotion to music, the world had given him only what he desired of it. He had reason enough to be content.

A passing labourer wished him good afternoon, and glanced at him with quick, sharp curiosity when he replied. They distrust us, he thought. They distrust the Germans, and one can't blame them. But they don't realize that we distrust them, too. Dresden in ruins . . . The opera-house gone; no longer any refuge for the shades of Weber and Wagner and Strauss. But Strauss was alive. He was at Garmisch. He had had an operation. Perhaps he would welcome a visit from someone with the same background, the same memories, as himself . . . Were there still pigeons on the *Brühlsche Terrasse*? The long, thick black poles at the corners of the Post Platz, each surmounted with its tiny gold swastika, would have been taken down. No loss . . . Hot chocolate in a restaurant in the Neu Markt, and Frieda listening in insolent silence while he talked of the opera. One evening she had admitted him to her bed. He had been clumsy, it had been a failure, but that hardly mattered now, any more than three years of near-starvation during the slump mattered. He would have enough to eat until he died . . .

Edwin Shorthouse is dead, he thought, the dismembered fragments of his body decorously reassembled in the coffin. He will cause no more trouble, and that is good and right and proper.

Judith Stapleton turned the corner by the New Bodleian and began to walk down Parks Road. At a discreet distance a man followed her. She went slowly, with bent shoulders and eyes grown ugly with crying. Presently she came to the

Radcliffe Science Building, and climbed the stairs to the library. The librarian looked up as she entered.

'Is it possible for me to use the library?' she said.

'Are you a science student?'

'No.'

'In that case I can only give permission if you're a graduate.'

'I am a graduate,' Judith lied.

'I see. Will you write down your name, degree, and college in this book?'

Judith wrote: 'Ann Matthews, B.A., St Hilda's.'

'I want the section on forensic medicine,' she said.

'Straight through, second bay on your right.'

'Thank you.'

There were very few other people in the library. Judith took down a standard text-book, settled down at a table, and looked up the article on food poisoning. Over this she spent some time, but without obtaining any satisfaction from it. Idly she turned back the pages, until some words in the section on arsenic caught her eye.

'*There is a progressive cachexia and loss of flesh,*' she read, '*due to malnutrition and physical and mental fatigue. The tongue is usually furred, or may be red and irritable. There is often an irritative condition of the fauces which causes constant hawking and laryngitis. The eyes are suffused and watery, the conjunctiva red-dened and smarting, and the lids may be puffy.*

'*Gastric irritability with attacks of vomiting and diarrhoea are common, and there is usually loss of appetite and distaste for food . . . An eczematous condition of the skin, pigmentation, and keratosis of the palms and soles may be observed. A white band sometimes may be noticed crossing the nails of the fingers and toes.*

'*Nervous symptoms may be pronounced or only slightly developed. Numbness and tingling of the hands and feet, accompanied by tenderness, and tenderness of the muscles are first complained of. These symptoms of peripheral neuritis are followed by atrophy of the muscles and paresis or paralysis.*'

After a moment's hesitation, Judith turned to the paragraphs on 'Methods of Administration'. The man who had followed her down Parks Road, and who had spent some seconds in examining the library register before entering the room, pushed by at the back of her chair to take down a volume from the shelves behind her. But she did not look up.

Boris Stapleton lay on his back, naked on a laboratory table. From a long gash in his abdomen a young doctor, wearing rubber gloves, was carefully removing the stomach and intestines. There was a strong smell of ether in the room, but it was insufficient to offset the effects of opening the body.

'Lord,' said the young doctor, 'how these cadavers stink.'

An older man, who was working at a bench nearby, frowned momentarily.

'For God's sake,' he remarked, 'remember that the poor devil was as alive as you are twenty-four hours ago.'

'Ah,' said the young doctor. 'A good deal can happen in twenty-four hours.' He made the last cut. 'Here we are. The Marsh test, or the Reinsch?'

At about five o'clock, the hotel porter brought Adam a note which a small and grubby boy had just delivered.

'*Meet me as soon as you are able,*' it ran, '*in Judith's room. First floor, second on the right. This is urgent.*' It was signed

187

'G.F.' Adam did not pause to reflect that he had never yet seen a sample of Fen's handwriting. He hesitated, and then went upstairs to the bedroom. Elizabeth opened the door to him. He saw that she had been crying.

'I've just come to tell you,' he said awkwardly, 'that I've got to go and meet Fen at Judith's digs. Afterwards I shall go straight to the theatre.'

'I see.'

'You'll be at the show, of course?'

'I don't know.'

'If you are, come to my dressing-room afterwards . . . Elizabeth, I'm sorry.'

She said nothing. Presently he turned and left the room.

Chapter Twenty-Two

Gervase Fen ate a large tea, lit a pipe, and retired to his study, intimating severely that no one was to disturb him. He had decided that he must make one last attempt to get to grips with the case. His failure to make anything of it thus far constituted a disagreeable mental irritant and made concentration on other matters difficult or even impossible. For his own sake, therefore, the business must be cleared up.

He settled down in an armchair by the fire and devoted his mind to a steady review of the material evidence. It proved unenlightening. He turned to opportunity: Joan Davis, Karl Wolzogen, Charles Shorthouse, Beatrix, Boris Stapleton, Judith, even Adam or Elizabeth – all had been alone at the time when Edwin Shorthouse met his death, and any one of them, presumably, could have been responsible for it. Yet for Stapleton's murder, only Judith, to all seeming, had had the opportunity, and he persisted in regarding her as innocent. The attack on Elizabeth could have been made by anyone except Adam, Charles Shorthouse, and Beatrix Thorn . . . But why had she been attacked at all?

Fen had a remarkable memory for detail. He began to re-enact, in imagination, every conversation and interview he had had since the case began. The process was long and troublesome, but at the end of it he had the truth.

It depended on three casual remarks: one made by Elizabeth in the 'Bird and Baby' on the morning after the murder, another made by Adam on the same occasion, and another made by Judith at the theatre. The last two, linked together and combined with a part of Elizabeth's information about the quarrel between Adam and Edwin Shorthouse, cleared up the problem of Stapleton's death. The first suggested a reason for the attack on Elizabeth and also a means by which Shorthouse might have met his end. Fen considered the topography of Shorthouse's dressing-room, and of its surroundings, and saw that these fitted well enough. There was one small fact, however, which refused to be assimilated, and on this he meditated for a considerable time. At last he smiled.

'Camouflage,' he said aloud. 'And confirmation, if one needed any. Now let me see . . .'

He spent some minutes browsing in medical books taken from his loaded and untidy shelves, and a rather longer period playing games with a cardboard box, some string, and other more or less symbolical objects. In the end he had no doubts. The method of each murder indicated the murderer beyond question.

The clock on the mantelpiece stood at a quarter to six. There was just time to communicate his results to Mudge before going on to the opera. He telephoned the police station.

'I've got the answer,' he said as soon as the Inspector was on the line. 'But it takes rather a lot of explaining, so I'd better come and see you. Is that all right?'

'If you *do* know, sir, I shall be eternally grateful.'

'Then prepare,' said Fen sternly, 'to be eternally grateful . . .

By the way, it wasn't Judith Stapleton who murdered her husband.'

'No?' Mudge sounded disappointed. 'Well, I'll be the judge of that when I hear what you have to say . . . I've had a man tailing her, you know.'

'How melodramatic.'

'It seems the last thing she did was to register under a false name at the Radcliffe Science Library.'

'Did she, now?' said Fen. 'Most reprehensible, I'm sure. I'll be with you shortly.'

He rang off and went up to his bedroom, where he devoted five flurried minutes to changing. Then he put on an overcoat and his extraordinary hat and went out to the garage. He was almost at the door of it when a horrifying thought suddenly occurred to him.

'Oh, my dear paws!' he exclaimed, and fled back to the telephone.

'Put me through,' he said, when at last the 'Mace and Sceptre' announced itself, 'to room 72.' He fretted and fidgeted until at last Elizabeth answered.

'Elizabeth?' he said. 'This is Fen. Is Adam with you?'

'No.' Elizabeth was surprised. 'I thought he was with you.'

'Well, he isn't,' said Fen grimly. 'Do you know where he was supposed to be meeting me?'

'At Judith's digs. But why—'

Fen, however, had no time to answer questions. He threw the telephone back on to the desk, fell over the cat, recovered himself, pounded into the hall, snatched an automatic pistol from a table drawer, and once again made for the garage.

'Now, Lily Christine,' he muttered, 'you can do something for your living.'

In this, unfortunately, he proved to be over-optimistic.

Nothing he could contrive would start the car. He tampered with the levers, and wound the handle, until he was exhausted. Finally, in an access of vengeful fury, he hurled an empty petrol-can at the chromium nude on the radiator-cap, seized his wife's bicycle, and wobbled frantically away on it.

Owing to a series of minor vexations and delays, it was twenty-five minutes past five before Adam arrived at the house in Clarendon Street, and he reflected, as he paused to look up at its windows, that he must be at the opera-house, in order to change and put on his make-up, by six o'clock at the latest. The house, which was Victorian in a mellow, Betjemanian fashion, stood back a little from the road. To reach the front door, whose brass handle shone brightly in a setting of flaky, ulcerated brown paint, one climbed three shallow steps of crumbling brick, passed through a small iron gate which stood permanently open, and walked up an asphalt path through a rather ravaged and desolate little garden. Adam, who had never accustomed himself to marching unheralded into lodging-houses, knocked and rang politely. But although he repeated this process a minute later, there was no sound or movement from inside; apparently the house was untenanted.

It was likely, Adam thought, that Fen had grown tired of waiting, and left. All the same, he had better investigate. '*First floor, second on the right . . .*' He opened the front door, went up the narrow stairs with their hard, thin carpet, and knocked at the appropriate door. Again there was no reply. With some hesitation, he opened the door and peered into the room. Though sparsely and cheaply furnished it was yet unexpectedly large. Clothes lay about it in confusion. On the end of the bed was a half-packed suitcase. A variety of rubbish had overflowed the waste-paper basket on to the floor around it. The windows, which were closed, had scanty yellow curtains. There was a gas-fire . . . Adam stepped into the room, and at this, as the result of a hard and well-aimed blow on the back of the head, all perception of his surroundings abruptly ceased.

After a time, a thin trickle of gas began to escape from the gas-fire, and the bedroom door was quietly closed, and locked on the outside.

Beatrix Thorn, the Master, Sir Richard Freeman, and Mr Levi all arrived at the opera-house at about ten minutes past six. The last two, though unacquainted, came together in the bar.

'I tell you, this Peacock 'e's good,' said Mr Levi. ''E 'ave them bums in the orchestra *genau* where 'e want 'em. We'll see something tonight, I'm warning you.'

Near them, a group of Young Intellectuals were discussing Wagner.

'Of course, the effect of the Teutonic gods and heroes of the *Ring* on the German mentality has been deplorable.'

'Exactly what I always maintain. In the last analysis, Wagner is responsible for Belsen.'

'I don't see how he can have been,' objected a dark-haired girl, 'considering he died several years before Hiltler was born.'

'Don't be deliberately obtuse, Anthea . . . *Die Meistersinger* is infected too, though in a more insidious and subtle way.'

'Yes. Cecil Gray says, you remember, that it's a great hymn to Germany's achievements in art and war.'

'There's only one mention of war in it,' said the dark-haired girl, 'and that's where Sachs says at the end that if Germany's ever defeated her art won't recover from it.'

They gazed at her with great dislike.

'Surely, Anthea, you're not maintaining that you know more about Wagner than Cecil Gray does?'

'Yes,' said the dark-haired girl simply, 'I am. But of course if you interpret Sachs' remark as a great hymn to German achievements in war, you're capable of believing anything.'

'And then there are the plagiarisms. There's that tune in the first scene of the last act which he cribbed from Nicolai's *Merry Wives*.'

'He didn't crib it from anything,' said the dark-haired girl. 'It's a variation on part of the Prize song.'

'. . . Moreover, it's obvious that a man of Wagner's moral character couldn't have produced great art. He was unscrupulous about money, he had affairs with the wives of his benefactors . . .'

'I don't see,' said the dark-haired girl, 'what moral character has to do with being able to produce great art. Villon was a thief, Bacon fawned for office, Tchaikovsky and Michelangelo were perverts, Gluck died of drink, Wordsworth was vain . . .'

'Oh, Anthea, don't be such a bore.'

Beatrix Thorn and the Master were still arguing about cars.

'And then the vibration . . . The structure of your ear . . .'

'I know nothing about the structure of my ear, Beatrix, and I don't wish to learn.'

'These undergraduates,' said Mr Levi cheerfully, 'they're a set of silly punks, *nicht wahr*?'

Chapter Twenty-Three

Fen arived at the house in Clarendon Street at about ten minutes past six, and was dismayed to find all the doors locked. He returned to the gate and gazed fretfully up and down the almost deserted road. A seedy-looking little man, who for some moments had been contemplating him with interest from the pavement, said:

'What's up, mate? Lorst yer key?'

'I can't get in,' said Fen dismally. 'I can't get in.'

''Eave a 'alf-brick through the winder,' the seedy little man suggested.

'I haven't got a half-brick.'

'No,' said the seedy little man with a *farouche* wink, 'but I 'ave.' He produced one from the pocket of his overcoat.

Fen seized it from him and was about to precipitate it through a front window when the little man, dismayed at such an intemperate and amateurish scheme, caught his arm.

'Not 'ere,' he said. 'Rahnd the back.'

They went round to the back and made an entrance through the kitchen window. Fen led the way up the stairs.

'Doesn't look to me,' said the little man disapprovingly, 'as if there's anything worth pinchin' 'ere. What we want is

socialism, so as everyone 'll 'ave some think worth pinchin' . . .
Phew, what a stink o' gas.'

In this he did not exaggerate. Fen rattled unavailingly at
the door behind which Adam lay. Then took several steps
back and hurled himself violently and uselessly against it.
The little man watched these injudicious goings-on with great
contempt.

'All you'll do,' he announced, 'is break yer collar-bone.'

'I believe I have broken it,' Fen complained.

''Ere,' said the little man. 'Let me get at it.' He took a
bunch of skeleton keys from inside his coat.

'You ought to be in prison,' said Fen amiably.

'Bloody good thing for you I ain't . . . Ah. That's done it.
Silly little lock, if you ask me. A child could pick it.'

They got Adam out of the room and into the open air.
He had recovered from the blow on his head, and had not
yet succumbed to the gas, the flow of which, owing to some
defect in the fire, was very weak. But he felt decidedly ill.
They held his head while he vomited.

'Tryin' ter take yer own life,' said the little man reproachfully. 'Ungodly, that's what it is.

'Think of the nice birds,' he added encouragingly, 'and the
nice trees, and the nice bloody atom bombs, and all the
things what make life worth living.' Having made this suggestion, he departed.

The fact that Adam's absence from the opera-house was not
discovered until the overture was actually under way was
not in itself surprising, for it was generally assumed, in so
far as anyone thought about it at all, that he had arrived
unnoticed and gone straight to his dressing-room. In the end
it was Joan who was responsible for the news. Rousing

herself from an agreeable day-dream at the call-boy's cry of 'Act one beginners, please,' she looked into Adam's dressing-room on her way downstairs, found it empty, thought for a moment that he had preceded her to the stage, and then saw his act one costume draped tidily over the back of a chair. This spectacle sent her running frantically downstairs to Karl Wolzogen.

'Karl!' she exclaimed. 'Where's Adam?'

He failed at first to appreciate the situation. 'How do I know where he is?' he said testily.

'You don't understand . . . *He's not in the theatre.*'

'What?' Karl was incredulous, alarmed.

'He's just not here.'

Karl stared at her blankly for a moment. '*Lieber Gott,*' he whispered. 'What are we to do?'

'I don't care,' said Adam obstinately. '*I must go and sing.*'

Fen attempted to dissuade him. 'After what you've been through,' he said, 'you're quite incapable of standing up and bawling your way through a five-hour opera.'

'I must try, that's all.'

'I suppose if you insist . . . By the way, you didn't see the person who hit you?'

'No.'

'I thought not,' said Fen, undismayed. 'But it was just as well to ask.' He perceived that across the road there was the shop of a dispensing chemist, and that it was still open. 'Come over here,' he said, taking Adam by the arm, 'and I'll get you some dope to help you keep going.'

The only occupant of the shop, which was small and overcrowded, was the chemist himself, a bald, paunchy, apprehensive middle-aged man.

'Make this up,' said Fen, and uttered technicalities. His knowledge of science, though inaccurate, was varied and occasionally useful.

'Have you a doctor's prescription, sir?'

'No.'

'Then I'm afraid it can't be done.'

'Oh, yes, it can,' said Fen, producing his automatic pistol. 'And if you don't get on with it at once, I shall shoot you, rather horribly, in the lungs.'

The chemist went very pale and put up his hands.

'I didn't ask you to do that,' said Fen, peeved. 'You can't make up a prescription standing in that attitude.'

He watched the chemist, issuing periodic instructions, as the man went to work. The result was a colourless liquid in a small glass, which Fen handed to Adam. Adam, who had hitherto been too bemused to question these extraordinary proceedings, now lost confidence.

'Is this stuff all right?' he demanded.

'Perfectly. And for heaven's sake hurry up. It's nearly half past six now.'

Adam mustered his resolution and swallowed the draught. It made him feel better almost at once.

'I hope to God,' he said, 'that they discovered fairly early that I wasn't there.'

'Take my wife's bicycle,' Fen suggested. He put the pistol back in his pocket and went outside to watch Adam pedal away.

After a moment the chemist came to the door of his shop. He did not at first observe that Fen was still in the immediate neighbourhood.

'Help, help,' he said to a surprised passer-by. 'Help.'

Fen was annoyed. 'Be quiet,' he told the chemist sternly.

'And don't be such a silly little man.' The chemist moaned with fear and rushed back into his shop. Greatly pleased at his previously unsuspected power of provoking terror in the breast of a fellow-being, Fen strode away.

Adam was horrified, when he arrived at the opera-house, to hear the music of the overture. It was about two-thirds of the way through, which meant, he calculated, that he had three minutes at the most to get changed and on to the stage. A concourse of incoherently agitated people met him. He forced his way past them and ran up the stairs, pulling off his coat. A belated lady of the chorus was startled to see him rushing towards her in the act of unbuttoning his trousers, and pressed herself against the wall, emitting faint, defensive screams, until he had gone by. There was no time for make-up – and of course the clothes were displaying that malevolent unmanageability with which they always reward anyone who is in a hurry to don or doff them. But somehow he got ready, and raced downstairs again, and was at his place as the penultimate chord of the overture sounded from beyond the curtain. He waved incautiously at Joan, and on this bravura gesture – which struck most of the audience as a singularly unhappy innovation – the curtain went up.

Fen found a telephone box and rang up Mudge.
'I'm sorry I wasn't able to get to you,' he said, 'but there have been fun and games.'
'Fun and games?'
'I'll explain later . . . I want you to send a couple of men backstage at the opera, because there may be an attempt to kill Langley.'

'*Langley?*'

'Yes. And come there yourself as soon as you can. By the way, you'll probably be getting some reports about me before long. I threw a brick at a window and threatened to shoot a chemist.'

'*Brick?*' Mudge said confusedly. 'Chemist?'

'Do stop repeating everything I say . . . I'll see you later. We'd better have a conclave after the performance. Bring that skeleton along, will you? – or anyway, *a* skeleton.'

He rang off and walked to the opera-house, where he watched the first act from the wings. The performance, quite evidently, was going well. Mudge's men arrived shortly after him, and he communicated certain possibilities to them. The Inspector himself, they said, would not be able to get away until later.

When the act was over, Fen after congratulating a cheerful and light-hearted cast, obtained a piece of information from Adam. Acting on this, he later searched one of the dressing-rooms, and, having found what he expected to find, took a taxi back to his home, where he 'retired to the attic' – an improvised laboratory – to make certain experiments. His family, who had learned from experience that Fen's experiments were often explosive and always malodorous, retired to the kitchen for mutual solace and reassurance.

For about two hours Fen occupied himself with hydrochloric acid, water, a strip of copper-foil, a Bunsen burner, and a small sublimation tube. Finally he inspected the results of his work through a microscope, and was pleased, though scarcely surprised, to find his hypothesis confirmed. He returned to the theatre just in time to witness the event which brought Mr Levi backstage in a condition nearing apoplexy, and cursing vividly in several remote tongues.

The opera had about twenty minutes to run. Adam chanting the splendours of the Prize Song, became obscurely aware, during one of the choral comments which punctuate it, that in some manner all was not well. He risked a glance into the wings, and saw that a revolver was levelled at him.

What followed took the audience very much by surprise. Herr Walther von Stolzing, apparently becoming belatedly aware that marriage to Eva might not be quite the ecstatic thing which fiction so gaily postulates, abandoned the Prize Song in mid-career, gazed wildly about him, and after a moment, descending from his mound, fled incontinently from the stage. Almost immediately there ensued a violent detonation – to which the carefully-planned acoustics of the theatre gave full effect – and a sound of scuffling and shouting from the wings. The cast stood rigid with amazement. There was a moment's uncertainty and then the curtain was lowered.

Mr Levi was with difficulty dissuaded from addressing the audience, whose mystification his words would most probably have deepened rather than allayed. In about five minutes the curtain rose again, and the opera was played through from the beginning of the Prize Song to the final chord. But there was no longer any spirit in it. Too many people had seen the attempt to kill Adam. Too many people had seen Judith, her features twisted with rage, and hatred, dragged away by the Inspector's men.

Chapter Twenty-Four

The interval during which the cast changed and removed make-up was occupied by Fen in explaining matters to Sir Richard Freeman and to Mudge, who had arrived opportunely during the rather uncertain applause. At about a quarter past eleven Adam, Joan, Peacock, Karl, Charles Shorthouse, Beatrix Thorn, and Elizabeth, who had after all been present at the performance, assembled in the green-room. The first four were exhausted, and spoke of Judith in low voices. The Master approached Adam.

'Ah, Langley,' he said amiably. 'How very trying all this is. I was virtually *ordered* to present myself here . . . By the way, I should like you to sing Aegistheus in the New York production of my *Oresteia*. You or Melchior. Can that be managed, I wonder?'

Adam had endured much that evening; he found himself, for the moment, incapable of replying.

Presently Fen appeared, with Mudge and Sir Richard Freeman. A silence fell. Through it Elizabeth, who remained unacquainted with the Master and Beatrix Thorn, and whom no one had so far enlightened as to their identity, could be heard saying innocently:

'But I thought Charles Shorthouse lived with some awful woman called Beatrix Thorn?'

Fen coughed noisily. 'Here is Miss Thorn,' he anounced; and added, with great severity: 'In the flesh.'

Elizabeth blushed, and Beatrix Thorn's face grew murderous. Fen hastened to cover the general embarrassment.

'There seems to be an impression among you,' he said 'that Judith was responsible for the deaths of Edwin Shorthouse and of her husband. You may as well know at once that that is not so.'

He watched their faces as he spoke. Adam was sprawling in a chair. Near him was Peacock, still in full evening dress, but wan and almost incapable of movement. Charles Shorthouse, wearing a black coat and with his black Homburg hat crammed rakishly on to his head, stood incuriously, his hands in his pockets, with Beatrix Thorn small and vehement, at his side. Joan Davis, neat, worldly and self-possessed, was with Elizabeth. Another silence ensued, longer and more intense than the first. Adam broke it by saying:

'But she tried twice to kill me. Why?'

'That's very simple, my dear Adam,' Fen replied in a curious voice. 'Very simple indeed. She tried to kill you because she hated you. And she hated you because she knew, even before we did, that it was you who killed her husband.'

Adam Langley went very white. His hair was tousled, and there was sweat on his forehead. He got to his feet. Elizabeth crossed the room, and took his hand in hers.

'I suppose,' said Adam thickly, 'that you also think it was I who killed Edwin Shorthouse?'

'Oh, yes.' There was no hint of joking in the way Fen spoke. 'You killed him too.'

'You fool,' said Elizabeth in a low voice. 'You damned fool.'

'This afternoon,' Fen went on, 'Judith visited the Radcliffe Science Library. She may have had shadowy suspicions before. But what she found, in a text-book of forensic medicine, amply confirmed them. She learned that arsenic could be administered externally, through the skin. She remembered that Boris had been practising make-up, for an hour every day. And she remembered, too, that he had been using a jar of removing-cream which you, my dear Adam, had given him. So this afternoon she got you, by a false message, to her room, and tried to gas you there, choosing a time when no one else would be in the house. If Mudge hadn't happened to mention to me, quite casually, that she'd visited the Science Library, she would probably have succeeded. But having failed, she made a second attempt – with, I may add, the gun which you so carelessly left in an unlocked drawer in your dressing-room. She was, as they say, "mad with grief"; which is a conventional phrase we use to describe a very horrible reality.'

Fen became suddenly matter-of-fact and cheerful, and in that electric atmosphere his change of manner was a shock. 'However,' he continued, 'I mustn't alarm you unduly. I mean what I say, of course. You *did* kill both those men. Two traps were set, and by a curious irony you quite unknowingly sprang both of them. I may add that one of them was set for you.'

Adam gulped. The colour flooded back to Elizabeth's face, and she began, almost unnoticeably, to cry with relief. Fen, observing this, experienced a twinge of conscience.

'Now, now,' he said ineffectually. 'Now, now.'

'Two traps . . .' Adam stammered.

Fen glanced at the others. 'Yes. There are two murderers in this case.'

'*For God's sake*,' said Peacock suddenly. His hands were trembling uncontrollably.

'And both of them,' Fen went on quietly, 'are dead.'

'Shorthouse and Stapleton!' Adam exclaimed.

'Certainly. Stapleton murdered Shorthouse. And Shorthouse, intending to kill *you*, murdered Stapleton. It's a curiously ironic situation – isn't it? That Shorthouse should revenge himself after his death.'

'But – but what about the attacks on me?' Elizabeth demanded.

'They were made, of course, by Stapleton, because of a remark you made in the "Bird and Baby" the other morning. You said, referring to the manner of Shorthouse's death: "*It's as though the laws of gravity were suspended*".'

'I still don't see . . .'

'I'll show you in a minute just how that applies. Let's first of all clear up the loose ends in the Stapleton murder. I was convinced from the first that Judith hadn't done it; she was too much in love with him for such an explanation to be conceivable. But apparently she was the only person who had the slightest opportunity of regularly doping his food or drink. Plainly, then, the arsenic must have been administered in some other way, and rather belatedly I remembered that it has effect if applied externally – for example, there are quite well-known instances of poisoning as the result of arsenic in face-cream, depilatories, soap, and so forth. Thinking back, I recollected that Stapleton was practising make-up – Judith herself told me so – and further, that in the "Bird and Baby" I heard that Adam had lent a jar of removing-cream to him. This evening, after inquiring what brand it was, I searched for it in the chorus dressing-room, and having found it, took it home and applied the Reinsch test. Even in the small amount which remained I found a good deal of powdered white arsenic. So evidently Stapleton had, in a sense, killed himself.

'Naturally, my first suspicion was of you, Adam. But I couldn't see, in the first place, why, if you were guilty, you had been so frank and open about giving him the removing-cream, and in the second place, why should you have wanted to kill him at all. You'd never met him before this production; you apparently weren't jealous of him on account of Judith; in fact, there seemed to be no possible advantage which you could get from his death. So unless you were some kind of homicidal maniac, or a disinterested killer like the man in Aiken's *King Coffin*, the explanation had to be sought elsewhere.

'It wasn't difficult to find. When Shorthouse visited your dressing-room during *Don Pasquale*, you came upon him meddling with the removing-cream. Actually he was substituting the poisoned cream for your own, since he still hated you as the result of your marriage with Elizabeth. It's small wonder that you thought his apology unconvincing . . . It wasn't a bad plot – though intended, I fancy, to hurt rather than kill, since he must have known that as soon as the stuff made you really ill you'd go to a doctor. For him, of course, it was a most unlucky chance that you caught him with the poisoned cream in his hand. If he attempted to restore the original jar you would naturally be suspicious, while if he didn't you would be even more suspicious when the symptoms began to show. There's only one thing I don't understand, and that's why he didn't *subsequently* remove the poisoned jar and put the other back.'

'That's easily explained,' said Adam. 'After I discovered him playing about in my dressing-room, I decided to keep it locked unless I was actually in it myself.'

'Ah. Then I think he must have been considerably relieved – though also, I suppose, puzzled – when this unpleasant scheme hadn't any results.'

'Thanks to Elizabeth,' Adam interrupted. 'If she hadn't that day bought me a superior brand of cream, and if I hadn't started at once to use it in place of the other, things would have become unpleasant . . . Though I might have saved Stapleton's life,' he added thoughtfully.

'Only temporarily,' said Fen. 'If he hadn't died of arsenic poisoning, he would have been hanged . . . I should add for the sake of completeness that I did just consider the possibility that Adam had killed Stapleton because Stapleton knew that Adam was guilty of Shorthouse's murder. But apparently the poisoning had begun *before* Shorthouse died – and in any case, it was soon obvious that Stapleton, and Stapleton alone, must have killed Shorthouse.'

Adam spoke hesitantly, 'You said that I—'

'You sprang the trap. But it was Stapleton who set it.'

Karl Wolzogen voiced the query that was in all their minds. 'But how was this thing done?'

'Come upstairs,' said Fen, 'and I'll show you. Mudge, will you prepare the scene?'

Chapter Twenty-Five

Ten minutes later they had all crowded, somewhat uncomfortably, into Edwin Shorthouse's dressing-room.

'As regards Judith,' Sir Richard said to Adam, 'we shan't, if you don't mind, prefer any charges. She'll recover more quickly at home with her parents than in any sort of mental institution. And once she knows the truth, there'll be no further danger to you.'

Charles Shorthouse spoke cautiously. 'I feel,' he announced, 'that this is in all probability a portentous moment, but I must confess that at present the exact meaning of it all eludes me . . .'

'If you feel tired, Master,' said his paramour, 'you must lie down.'

'No.'

'It doesn't do to exhaust yourself.'

'Kindly be silent, Beatrix.'

Mudge was fussing with the skeleton which had been found in the property-room; Adam noticed that the wire which held together the cervical vertebrae had been straightened. On the floor lay three lengths of rope and some cotton waste. Fen assumed a didactic expression and called for silence.

'Now, we know,' he said, '*why* Stapleton intended to kill

Edwin Shorthouse. It was because of the attempted rape of Judith Haynes. But you must realize that he'd no intention of being connected with the crime if he could possibly help it, and so, having a twisted and ingenious mind, he conceived a twisted and ingenious plan. That plan he tested, in advance, with this skeleton.

'His first job was to screw that hook in the ceiling – the one from which we found Edwin Shorthouse hanging. There would, of course, be plenty of opportunity for that, and the only danger was that Shorthouse would notice the thing. Even if he did, however, he could hardly suspect its purpose.

'Stapleton's next step was to steal the Nembutal which he knew was in Joan's dressing-room, and to dope the gin which Shorthouse kept in here, and it was over this that he made his one mistake. The Nembutal had, of course, to be put in the *bottle*, where it would certainly arouse suspicion if found. I think there's no doubt that he intended to rearrange that part of his setting – by substituting an innocuous bottle for the doped one – while he was in here, *and that when it came to the point, he forgot*. It's the dreariest of platitudes to say that every murderer makes at least one mistake, but unlike most platitudes, that one happens to be true.

'Well, then; as usual, Shorthouse comes up here to drink after he's finished his round of the pubs. Stapleton waits until it's safe to assume that the drug has taken effect, and then goes up to the roof above here, with a good length of rope. On the way, he makes sure that the lift is at the second and not at the ground floor. He knows that Furbelow, being in fear of such contraptions, won't touch it, and he doesn't expect anyone else to be in the theatre at that late hour. The machinery of the lift, you'll remember, is not far from that skylight there.'

'Oh,' said Adam, suddenly enlightened.

'Yes, exactly,' Fen agreed. 'But of course if *you* hadn't taken the lift, *Stapleton* would have done so, so you needn't be unduly distressed. He must have been considerably startled when you did that part of his job for him.

'One end of his rope, then, he attaches to the machinery of the lift, or to the top of the lift itself. Its length has been nicely calculated, for he mustn't run the risk of pulling the unfortunate man's head off . . . The other end he takes with him to the little skylight. Through that skylight he drops into the room two further lengths of rope (unattached), some cotton waste, and the end of the rope which is attached to the lift. A stool of exactly the right height has been placed in the room previously. Immediately beside the skylight, on the roof, he fits up some temporary projection – perhaps a small nail. Have you done that, Mudge?'

'Yes, sir.'

'Good . . . Now he's ready. An appointment to discuss his opera score with Shorthouse has already been made, so as to minimize subsequent suspicions. He comes in here at five to eleven, observed by Furbelow, knowing perfectly well that nothing on earth will make the old man put his nose into the room while Shorthouse is there. And he makes his final arrangements . . . Mudge, go and drop a length of rope through the skylight, will you. You needn't bother to attach it to the lift, but hang on to your end, and heave away when I give the word.' Mudge departed on this errand. 'As you see,' Fen continued, 'the other materials are already here.'

In due time the rope appeared through the skylight, accompanied by a sound of muffled panting from Mudge.

'Now,' said Fen, 'observe what Stapleton does. The skeleton represents Shorthouse, now unconscious from the drug.'

He took a piece of chalk from his pocket, and with it very lightly marked two points on the seat of the stool. Then, holding it where the marks were, he carried the stool to the skeleton and pressed the bones of the fingers and thumb against the wood in several carefully selected places.

'We now have fingerprints,' he said, 'appropriate to the theory of suicide.'

Putting the stool aside, he picked up the shorter length of rope from the floor, stood on a chair, and tied one end of it firmly to the hook in the ceiling. The other end he arranged in a running noose, with a knot placed where the angle of the jaw would be. Then he climbed down, took the longer piece of rope, tied it round the wrists of the skeleton, and after a moment untied it again.

'What on earth . . . ?' said Adam, mystified.

'Ah,' said Fen. 'That took me in, too. You see, Stapleton's plan involved tying Shorthouse's *ankles*, a fact which was quite impossible to conceal. The tying of the wrists too was merely a camouflage – the best he could devise. It wasn't bad, either. Anyway, it filled my head with quite a number of imbecile theories . . .'

He now fixed the longer rope around the waist of the skeleton, passed the free end over the hook and hauled. Drooping, the skeleton rose into the air. When it had reached a sufficient height, Fen tied his end of the rope to the door handle, took the stool, and adjusted it so that the feet of the skeleton rested on it. Then he again mounted his chair, and put the noose which hung from the ceiling about the neck. He inserted the cotton padding, and pulled the rope fairly tight.

'Suicides often like to make themselves comfortable,' he said indistinctly over his shoulder, 'which was a very good

211

thing for Stapleton. It was most important that Shorthouse should not be strangled prematurely.'

He climbed down and took away the rope from the skeleton's waist. It sagged forward, the feet resting on the stool, the neck supported from the hook in the ceiling.

'As you see, it needs a good deal of care,' said Fen. 'But *given* care, Shorthouse could live quite a long time, even suspended in that fashion. The real problem is to avoid pushing the tongue back against the pharyngeal wall, and also to avoid putting pressure on the carotid sinus and the vagus nerves. But you'll notice that quite a lot of weight is taken by the feet.'

He now took the end of the rope which was hanging through the skylight and fastened it round the skeleton's ankles, with the knot at the back. A handkerchief from his pocket served to remove his fingerprints from the chalk-marked places at which he had touched the stool. Finally, he untied the remaining length of rope from the door-knob and fastened it round one leg of the stool.

'This,' he announced, pink with effort, 'is a knot called the Highwayman's Hitch. You have to keep both ends in your hand. One of them will bear any amount of strain, but if you pull the other the whole knot comes undone.'

As he spoke, he was making rough loops in the two ends. With these in his hand, he climbed on to the chair for the last time, pushed them through the skylight, and hung them on the nail on the outside which Mudge had provided. The last thing he did was carefully to wipe the seat and back of the chair he had been using.

'Now,' he said, 'everything's ready. Stapleton leaves the room, and is conducted by Furbelow from the theatre. After a short interval he goes to a public box and telephones Dr Shand, saying that Shorthouse is in urgent need of medical

help – for he must have a medical witness on the spot immediately after he has sprung his trap, or all this effort is wasted:
that's to say, some reliable person must be there to swear
that Shorthouse had *only just* died – he died, in fact, long
after Stapleton left the dressing-room. Stapleton can calculate,
with some certainty, how long it will take Shand to get here
– and if *he's* not available, there are other doctors whose
addresses are in the telephone book. Then, just previous to
the psychological moment, he re-enters the theatre, intending
to lower the lift – only to find, my dear Adam, that you're
engaged in doing it for him.'

'Oh, Lord,' groaned Adam, 'if only I'd known . . .'

'But you didn't know,' said Fen, 'so there's no earthly use
worrying about it . . . Anyway, let's watch what happens
when the lift is lowered. Mudge is the lift for the purposes
of this test . . . Haul away, Mudge,' he called. 'Haul away,
oh, haul away.' He broke into a sea-shanty, but was silenced
by the Chief Constable.

The rope tied round the ankles of the skeleton tightened,
and in another moment, still suspended by the neck, its feet
were lifted from the stool and dragged upwards towards the
skylight. The back of the neck was pressed against the angle
of the ceiling, and when the feet were within an inch or
two of the skylight, there was a crack as one of the cervical
vertebrae gave way under the strain.

'Well, there we are,' said Fen. 'Mudge,' he called, 'can you
fasten the rope somewhere, and undo the knot at the ankles?'

'Right you are, sir,' came Mudge's disembodied answer.
And after a moment's pause his hand appeared through the
skylight, groped, found the knot, and loosened it. The skeleton swung down again like a pendulum, and the rope was
withdrawn.

'Hence his panic at your mention of suspending the laws of gravity,' Fen explained to Elizabeth. 'Hanging a man feet upwards is certainly rather phenomenal . . . Now the stool, Mudge.'

One strand of the rope attached to the stool was jerked, and it fell on its side; the other, and the Highwayman's Hitch came undone. ('That's lucky,' said Fen in mild surprise. 'I don't often get it right first time.') This rope vanished, like its predecessor, and they were alone in the room with a skeleton swinging from a hook.

'Neat,' said Fen with admiration. 'Complex but neat. Of course once one had grasped the *method*, the *culprit* was obvious. As you see, the arrangements have taken me about ten minutes – which means that even if some other person had entered the dressing-room while Furbelow was showing Stapleton off the premises, he or she would not have had time to fix the trap, since Furbelow was away only three minutes. Stapleton was helped, of course, by the fact that there were plenty of hiding-places about the theatre, and what's more, his plan couldn't have been carried out if it hadn't been for Furbelow's habit of staying up till midnight, and of sitting with the door of his room open in order to minimize the noxious gases from his electric fire. That was essential to Stapleton's alibi. After he'd dismantled his apparatus, he no doubt came down from the roof, and got away from the theatre, while Shand was in here with Furbelow . . . It's odd, though, to think that all the time he was dying of arsenic supplied by the man he was killing – and didn't know it.'

There was a long pause. Mudge could be heard clattering down the iron ladder from the roof. Elizabeth said to Adam: 'Darling, I've been intolerable. But now it's all over, I'll really try to behave myself. And I do love you so much.'

214

Peacock said to Joan:

'Levi's given me the job, my dear. Let's get married quickly.'

And in the place where, a week ago almost to the minute, Edwin Shorthouse had died, two couples embraced. Sir Richard began to display a marked interest in the litter of articles on the dressing-table. Fen, less discreet, looked on with an air of sentimental indulgence.

The Master, who had watched the entire proceedings open-mouthed, now spoke.

'Extraordinary,' he said. 'Very extraordinary and interesting. And how like Edwin to make a fuss and nuisance about even the simple act of dying. I won't say,' he added generously, 'that I've quite fathomed it all yet . . .'

'By the way,' said Fen, 'where did you and Miss Thorn go when you left Wilkes that evening?'

'Oh we never left him at all,' said the Master innocently. Then a spasm of annoyance passed over his face. 'There now – I shouldn't have said that.'

'Why not?' Fen asked, suddenly suspicious.

'I promised Wilkes,' said the Master naïvely. 'He rang up on the morning after my brother's death, and particularly asked me to say I had left him shortly before the time of the murder. I admit,' the Master went on unhappily, 'that his motives were not clear to me, but he was so insistent that I thought it would be discourteous to refuse. He mentioned, I believe, that it would have the effect of confusing you, though I cannot understand *why* . . .'

'I see,' said Fen with deep and inexpressible emotion. '*I see.*'

'But before you go, my dear fellow,' the Master pursued, 'we must have a word about the New York production of my *Oresteia.*'

'Surely you realize by now that I'm *not* the agent of the Metropolitan Opera House?'

'Nor you are.' The Master's countenance was sad. 'Well, never mind. I expect they wanted a younger man for the job. Better luck next time.' He grew more cheerful. 'I'll tell you what I'll do, though. I'll let you sell me that nice little car of yours.'

Anyone passing through the bar of the 'Mace and Sceptre' before lunch the following morning would have seen three people seated at a corner table. The girl, who was small and brown-haired, held an open note-book and a pencil, and there was an expression of unnatural gravity on her face. The younger of the two men sat gazing at his pint tankard with the greatest amiability. And the third member of the party was tall and lanky, with a ruddy, clean-shaven face and dark hair which stood up in rebellious spikes at the crown of his head. He held a glass of whisky, was frowning with the effort of concentration, and appeared to be making some oracular pronouncement. He said:

'The era of my greatest successes . . .'